# *Wildflowers In May*

# *Jasmine Styles*

Copyright © 2022 Jasmine Styles
All rights reserved

*To the woman who inspired me the most.
I will forever love and miss you, Nan.*

## Trigger Warnings:

This book contains adult themes such as violence, references to mental health issues, mentions of infertility and miscarriage and murder.
Reader discretion is advised

\*\*\*

Have you ever seen wildflowers in May?

The way they bloom so vividly in the light and the way they shine in the sweet spring rain.
The way their colours fill a space and bring the feeling of peace into wherever you keep them.

Have you ever smelt wildflowers in May?

The way their scent fills your nose and opens you mind.
The way it invites you into the world they bloom from.

Have you ever felt wildflowers in May?
The way the soft petals run through your fingertips.
The way they softly graze your skin as you walk by.

Have you ever seen wildflowers in May?

\*\*\*

## Chapter One

The rain drizzled steadily outside the window onto the dark worn pine of the front porch. Beading in the puddles as it drips down from the roof. The grey sky growing darker by the minute. The storm was coming early.
I gazed down into the pale blue teacup in my hands. The murky tea inside reflecting my tired face.
It was always so peaceful at this time of the morning. No one was awake but me. I welcomed the feeling of being alone just as I always had. It was quieter that way. Easier to breathe.
I stood from my spot on the windowsills cold wooden bench seat, never once taking my eyes off the surrounding thick greenery of the forest. It always looked beautiful in the rain. The thin morning mist only aiding to enhance the vibrant green of the tall grass and the deep colour of the leaves on the looming trees of the forest.
I raised my sweet tea to my lips and took a sip, the warm amber liquid heating my body with rich comfort.
My lips curling into a smile against the thick rim of the blue mug. The smallest things had always seemed to bring me joy. The way the tea warmed me in the bitterly freezing cold winter mornings before I started work for the day was up there with my very short list of favourite things.

I finished my hot beverage slowly and looked around the large open house, savouring the warmth on my tongue. The early morning sun's light bounced off the fading cream-coloured walls. The sunny yellow cushions beaming against the neutral pale brown furniture. Mum had always liked the colour yellow. I missed her more with each passing day lately.

My eyes caught a glimpse of the old wooden clock on the fading floral walls. Eight am. A groan left my throat at the thought of leaving my warm sanctuary and embracing the cold morning of the outside world.

I placed my cup in the deep white porcelain sink in the kitchen and filled it with water to soak. Hot steam swirled from the dirty cup.

I opened the front door quietly and raised the hood of my black winter jacket. The rain patted against my head gently as I walked to my car. My auburn hair beginning to frizz in the cool autumn drizzle. The gravel underneath me crunched with every step. Trees rustled in the early morning wind. The smell of rain entered my nose as I tried to hold my breath against the crisp stormy air.

I hurried to my car as the storm moved its way in. The faded red paintwork on the bonnet shone through the pale morning light. Clouds hung low over the sky, threatening their heavy wrath.

## Chapter Two

"Good morning, Marty!" Francis called from the register as I walked into the small bright café. The café was in the centre of our small town and was a very popular spot amongst the town's few residents. The cosy cottage like ambiance was like a warm welcome home to all who entered. The pale baby blue walls and white wooden tables adding to the home style feeling along with the fake plastic vines they had draped from the walls. The bold smell of coffee filling the crisp cool air.
"Good morning, Frank!" I called back, tying my black apron around my navy work pants. My damp jacket clinging to me with wetness as I pulled it off. I tightened my hair band and smoothed out the frizz that had formed.
"I think it will be a quiet one today, my little friend." Frank sighed, his gaze lingering out the front windows of the cafe. His short grey hair falling to the right as he slumped his small thinning head against his palm. I gave him a smile and began to work. As I stocked all the white paper takeaway cups for the day and filled the drink fridges out front of the café, I listened to the radio singing softly in the background. I found myself humming along to the soft pop song as it played its cheery tunes whilst the rain continued to fall steadily outside. The rain had begun to fall heavier. My gaze turned to the window to look out at the gloomy dark sky. Clouds crowding each other in a

dark marbling storm. It was hard to believe it was only nine in the morning.

The door chimed as a stranger opened it timidly.

I will never forget the moment I first laid eyes on him. His thick black hair curled against his face, damp from the falling rain. His deep blue eyes full of comfort and wonder as he entered somewhere warm, new and inviting. I watched his tall stature as he shrugged off his pale green windbreaker. I admired him from the corner of my eye as I stocked the cold fridge with fresh bottles of soft drink. He looked no older than me. I couldn't pull my attention away from him.

"Can I please just get a medium latte with one sugar to have here?" his voice was calming and smooth when he approached the counter.

"No worries. Name for that one?" Frank asked.

"Eric."

He spoke with such an air around him. A voice of someone who was very comfortable in their own skin. It had me hooked from the moment it fell upon my ears. My heart began to beat quickly against my chest.

"Marty?" Frank called over to me cheerfully. I turned my head and made my way quietly over to him behind the marble counter, avoiding the newcomers gaze. The lights began to flicker as thunder rumbled above us. "Would you mind fixing this coffee for me?" he asked with his thick greying eyebrows raised. He looked up at the high roof worriedly as if it were to drop at any sudden moment.

"Not at all." I took the smooth emerald mug from him and began to make the strong brew. Eric had sat himself at a table by the window gazing out as the rain began to fall even harder on the pavement. The sound of the downpour now echoing loudly through the small space.

I swallowed hard as I made my way over to him. My shoes padded slowly on the clean white tiled floor. He sat reading a vintage book dampened from the storm outside under the dim light from the tall, large front window.

"Here you are." I spoke shyly as I sat the deep green mug down in front of him on the simple white table.
"Thank you. It was Marty, wasn't it?" he smiled at me with a perfectly crooked smile.
"Yes." I smiled small back to him. The heat in my cheeks rising to my ears. My breath hitched sharply in my throat as I tried to swallow my sudden flow of anxiety.
"Interesting name for woman your age." He noted with his thick dark eyebrows raised. His sweet blue eyes glistening softly in the overhead fluorescent lights.
"It's short for Martha." I confessed bluntly. I hated my full name. Blood began to rush to my face. Regret filled my body at the sound of my tone.
"Well, it was lovely to meet you, Martha." He grinned at me again, ignoring my tone. My heart fluttered in my chest.
My smile grew bigger after he greeted me, I begun to feel myself relax.
The glass front door opened and closed with a slam. I jumped in fright at the loud bang from the heavy glass door. A small gasp escaped my lips.
"Blasted door." Greg thunderous voice mumbled as he tripped over his own feet.
Greg was my favourite regular customer we had come into the shop. He was a tall thin older gentleman whose skin was tanned and wrinkled from years of working in the outdoors. He knew it too. He always complained about having the complexion of an old oak tree.
"Good morning, Greg." I turned all my attention to him from Eric, relieved for the sudden distraction.
"Ah, there you are, my little love!" he opened his long arms as he took his usual seat by the left window.
"Just the usual today, Greg?" I asked him sweetly.
Flashing him a tender smile. Beads of rain peppered his bald head.
"What else do I ever order, my dear?" he grunted, stroking his white wiry moustache.
Whilst I prepared his strong black coffee, I gazed at Eric

finishing his reading of a section in his old damp book. I was fascinated by the way he moved so gracefully as he left the store without a word.
He turned back to me and gave me a small smile before heading out into the now heavily pouring rain.
"There's a horrible storm brewing out there." Greg noted, pointing a worn thumb to the window.
"Is it bad on the roads home?" I swallowed hard. The fear of having an accident crept over my body
"They are pretty slick today, my dear. You be safe out there. You hear me?" Greg wiggled a thin finger at me.
"I always am, Greg." My lungs heaving out a pent-up sigh.
"We don't want a repeat of what happened to your late mother." He said gruffly.
"No, we don't." I mumbled under my breath.

## Chapter Three

The workday ended up going quickly which was a surprise to both Frank and me. The storm had scared everyone into their homes so there was no one else that had come in that day.
"Come on now. Go home, Marty." Frank insisted as I leaned against the stone counter looking out at the empty town. The lonely streets awash with dirty water from the downpour.
"I'm alright, Frank. Honestly." I straightened. My back cracked loudly as I stood up straight and reached my hands above my head. Frank cringed at the noise. He hated when I cracked any part of my body. The simple sound was enough to make him gag.
"Well, I'm not alright with you driving all the way home in this storm. So, go on now. Before it gets worse. I won't have your blood on my hands." he ushered me out the door and toward the cold stormy road. I knew it was no use arguing with him, so I obeyed his command.
I untied my dirty coffee and cake-stained apron from my waist and dashed toward my red car out the front. The hood of my jacket providing little cover from the pouring rain. The car door creaked as I threw it open. Only for it to slam itself behind me in the wind as it howled down the empty street.

I sat in the car for a moment before driving home. The heater steadily getting warmer as the time passed. Lightning crashed and illuminated the dark sky. It looked a lot later than two in the afternoon. The windscreen wipers were smooth against the window as they wiped away the falling downpour.
The long road home was slick with rain. The tall green trees swinging in the harsh wind as it ripped through them. Leaves swirled in the harsh breeze and tumbled to the ground. The sky was hidden beneath a mass of dark grey storm clouds.
I drove slowly to avoid any accidents. I was always terrified of being involved in an accident after my mother's tragic one. The music was close to silent in the car to avoid any distractions. No one else was on the road. They would have been crazy to even consider going out in this storm.

As I drove up the long gravel driveway of my house, I noticed the only light on in the house was the living room. The only one I had left on before my shift this morning. Smoke billowed from the chimney.
"Thank god." I sighed to myself.
Dad must not have moved around the house much today. The rain had slowed its pour briefly. I knew it was only a matter of time before it started up again.
The large grey house loomed over the surrounding forest. My grand old house of secrets. I reached a hand to the cold brass door handle and turned it slowly to not startle dad.
"Dad?" I called once inside to let him know it was only me. My voice echoing down the dark silent hallway. I slid my shoes off and kicked them under the entry table, immediately feeling more comfortable. The scent of pine burning in the open fire opened my senses with more comfort. I loved the open fire. It reminded me of my mother and all the times we had sat together with me in her lap reading a picture book or her singing in my ear softly as watched the flames dance over the wood.

A sharp pang hit my chest at the memory. I ached to be able to sit with her just one more time.

All I had ever wanted was to make her proud.

"I'm here, kiddo." Dad's voice drew my longing gaze from the warm fire and down the hall to him. He sat at the large brown wooden kitchen table hunched over his work laptop.

Dad never liked going outside the house unless he absolutely had to. He was always inside and hidden away from anyone and everyone. 'Prying eyes', he called them. I sat opposite him at the dining table in my usual seat. His small gold rimmed glasses sat on the tip of his nose as he looked over his screen. His soft brown hair shining in the light. The oncome of grey hairs glistening against the dusty brown. His greying stubble poking through the mass of unkempt brown hair on his angular face.

"Horrible storm." I noted, breaking the thick silence between us.

"I was worried to death about you, Marty." he fretted. His glasses slid further down his crooked nose. His deep ocean blues glistening with worry. They narrowed down onto me, baring into my eyes.

"I'm fine dad." I smiled and reached my hands over to touch his strong ones either side of his laptop. They were warm to the touch against my cold ones. The warmth stung my freezing skin.

"You know how your mother died, Marty. I can't lose you like that too." The memory of my mother slipped into my mind. Her beautiful chestnut hair and her perfect loving smile. The way her hazel eyes used to light up when she looked at me. My heart filled with pain and a longing need to hold her again for just one more second. I loved my father with every fibre of my being, but he just wasn't the same.

When I was eleven, my mother was killed in a horrific accident. She didn't survive the ordeal. My father couldn't cope with the grief and the sorrow from other people in the town, so he became a recluse to the house. To everyone else, he went missing after the crash with many people believing he was involved in the accident somehow. Some going as far to say he did and then faked his death. Dad made me swear not to tell a single soul about him or his current whereabouts. Not one single soul could know he was still alive. He had spent just over twelve years in hiding. There were times where he would leave the house for business, but I had always been too afraid to question where he was going. Dad had always had a horrid temper. I had spent my teenage years being raised by my mother's sister Marion and her husband John. They took me in after the crash and raised me as if I were their own whilst dad couldn't be there.

They weren't allowed to know dad was hiding here in the house. Dad didn't want anyone at the house at all at any given time. I t was one of his many rules.

The house was always mine by right from mum's will but I wasn't allowed to move into it alone until I had turned eighteen so I spent my free time sneaking out of the house to see dad and bring him whatever leftovers and food I could get for him so he could eat something other than the food he had caught and foraged himself. Uncle John always looked after the house for me, making sure it was well maintained. He would look after the lawns and keep the inside tidy. They had a cleaner visit once a week to clean it for me. They never once found dad's hidden rooms under the house or his generators. My father was a very smart man.

"You won't lose me, Dad" I grabbed his hand and gave him a reassuring squeeze "I will always be your little girl." I smiled brightly at him.

He squeezed my hand back tightly.

"So how was work?" he asked, closing the silver laptop lid and transferring all of his attention to me.

"Work was work." I shrugged, pulling my hand away.

"No one interesting come in today?" he asked.

I shook my head. The image of Eric entered my head. Why

was I so enamoured by him? There was no way I could tell dad about him.

"What's for dinner?" I changed the subject quickly. Distracting myself from the thought of him.

"Well considering it is almost three pm and bucketing down outside, I was thinking of making a nice warm soup for dinner with some fresh crusty bread I made this morning. Any requests?" he smiled broadly. His blue eyes brimming with joy.

"Surprise me." I stood and kissed him on his wrinkled forehead. The warm spiced scent of his shampoo filled my nose and brought a wave of calm over me. My father meant everything to me. He was all I had left in this bleak existence.

"Can do, sweetheart." He smiled up at me.

I left him alone in the kitchen and headed up the stairs to my bedroom.

It was always bitterly cold inside the house where the fire didn't reach. Dad liked to keep the power bill as low as he possibly could, so he only turned on the inducted heater at night. He usually lit the wood fire in the living room though which was always so warm and comforting but the heat never really flowed upstairs.

Sometimes I like to think he just lights the downstairs fire so I that I would come and be near him.

I changed from my grubby work uniform into my soft winter pyjamas. The soft blue fleece welcoming me home.

"That is *not* what I had said…" dad's thundering voice echoed in the kitchen and faded outside with the slam of a door.

He was always having private talks outside on the back porch all the time, but I never knew with who. I didn't care to listen much either, believing it was easier that way.

The hard-wooden floors creaked under my feet as I made my way to the woodfire blazing downstairs. I sat in front of the open fire and opened my book. The old pages dusty smell filled me with a familiar comfort whilst a gentle smile crept across my face.

I lost track of time whilst I read the old novel.


The rain had slowed and had turned to a steady drizzle and the sky had lightened enough for rays to shine down during the late sunset. Dad had come back in but was working hard from his computer whilst I read alone in the cosy lounge room.

"Here you are, my darling." Dad handed me a deep porcelain bowl of pumpkin soup. The rim was cracked from years upon years of use.

The thick orange liquid steaming in the bowl stirred the silent hunger in my stomach as I begun to eat it.

The warm liquid slid down my throat as I took my first spoonful. Pumpkin was always the superior flavour in my opinion. Dad preferred tomato. It was an ongoing debate amongst the two of us.

Dad always made the best soup. Even though it was almost always from a can. He would add any spices he thought of and somehow, they would always work. He sat across from me on the dark woollen mat by the fire. He smiled from behind his chipped white bowl as he brought it to his lips. The liquid dripping onto his grey stubbled chin.

He kept my gaze as he devoured his soup.

I dropped my eyes back down to my book as he swallowed.

"What are you reading?"

"Just a fantasy novel." I tore my eyes from my page to look at him.

"Ahh." He dramatically sighed "About dragons?"

"Not quite." I laughed.

"Come on then. Tell me, Kiddo. What's it about?" He scooted closer to me on the floor.

"Just a love story with knights and monsters."

"Oh, interesting. A love story?"

"Not for me dad. You know I'm not interested in anyone."

I sighed whilst rolling my eyes.

"Good girl, Marty. You don't need a man." He cocked an eyebrow with concern.
"Yes, dad. I know." I groaned, closing the book and putting it down next to me, hoping the conversation would end.
"Are you working tomorrow?" he changed the subject happily. The tension hanging in the slowly dissipating.
I nodded, drinking my hot soup. The liquid burning my throat as it slid down.
"Where?" he asked.
"Eight am until two at the café and then three until seven at the store." I wiped my mouth on the back of my hand. The orange liquid staining my pale skin.
"Don't burn yourself out kid." He said worriedly, a small wrinkle appearing between his furrowed brows.
"I won't, dad." I said as I wiped my hand on my clean pants to rid it of the bright soup stain.
He sat his empty bowl down on the floor and looked at me. His soft eyes glinted with happiness. He stretched his body out on the floor before sitting back up to face me. He must have been stiff from working at the table all day.
"Would you be interested in watching a movie with your old man, Miss Green?" he smiled at me.
"What do you have in mind?" I smirked, putting my now empty bowl inside of his.
"Maybe something with dragons?" he matched my cheeky smirk.
"You're on!"

## Chapter Four

The small tone of my alarm roused me from my heavy sleep.
I groaned at the thought of leaving my warm bed. The birds had begun their usual morning song. Their high tweets echoing through the silent house.
I rolled out of bed and opened my white lace curtains, filling the room with a dim light from the sunrise. I could admire the sight for hours. The early morning sky flooding with pink and orange light as the sun rose from its slumber.
The warm water of the shower coated my body welcomingly as I turned the cold brass knob of the tap. The scent of my lavender body wash intoxicating me with its relaxing aroma. Time seemed to pass me by quickly this morning.
My café uniform was cold against my warm skin as I slid them over me. The smell of coffee stained into the worn cotton fabric.
The pastel flowers on the wallpaper of my room looked as if they were blooming in the early morning sun. Their soft colours dancing against the light cream background.
I fumbled around on the floor for a pair of fresh work clothes for the supermarket. I shoved them in a backpack and headed downstairs running my hand over the polished oak banisters.
"Time to eat I suppose." I sighed, looking in the pantry for

something appetising.
Nothing stuck out apart from a box of wheat flakes.
"That will do." I shrugged.
I ate my cold soggy wheat cereal quickly as I watched the endless ticking the clock. Seven thirty-five am.
My heart raced as I hurried to wash my bowl before heading into town for a long day of working.
The drive felt longer this morning than usual. We lived out of town in an old farm manor by a field, so it was always a fairly long drive as it was.
The field was my favourite place in the world. I always spent any free time I had laying amongst the luscious greenery and the blooming wildflowers. Loosing myself for a few moments among the earth.
The rain had eased off overnight which meant more people were around the small town. No one ever really left the town, and it wasn't very often anyone came here to stay permanently. The memory of the new boy entered my mind. His sweet smile and aura bringing a smile to my face. I had never actually been very interested in a boy let alone anyone else in this place. I wonder what he was doing here in such a small town.
The café was empty when I pulled up out the front. I locked my red truck and made my way inside.
"Good morning, my dear!" Frank called from beyond the back room as I opened the glass door for the invitingly warm breeze outside to blow inside. He always seemed to know when it was me entering the door without even having to look up from whatever it was, he was doing.
"Morning, Frankie!" I called back, slipping on my black apron over my navy-blue uniform.
Morning sunlight bounced vividly off the white tables scattered among the room. The soft hum of music played to dull the silence.
"Has anyone been in yet, Frank?" I called out to him.
"Been pretty busy this morning actually." Frank emerged from the back room rubbing his balding head.

"Why didn't you call me in earlier?" I asked as he walked past me to the bakery cabinet.
"You needed a little lay in, Martha." He smiled at me. I cringed at the sound of my real name. It made me feel like I was over sixty years old and well on my way to becoming a senior citizen.
"Thank you, Francis." I said through gritted teeth. He huffed at me saying his real name too.
"Would you mind cutting the cake from the back and putting it on the counter?" he asked, pointing at the back room behind him.
"Sure thing." I shrugged.
The fresh cake stood on a serving dish with a long knife next to it on the centre counter. Frank loved baking. He was forever sending me home with something new he had baked. I often wondered why he would look after me and why he gave me the job here above all the others that had applied. But deep down I always knew.

He knew my mother when she was young. She grew up in the town and lived her whole life here. She used to work in the café before it had burnt down and had to rebuild.
People in the town thought it was my father that had burnt it down out of spite. Not many people seemed to like him. But to me, he was my everything. He was the sweetest and smartest man I knew. People just liked to gossip too much. I think Frank was always secretly in love with my mother and the fact that she passed the way she did hurt him deeply. I always knew his taking in of me was in debt to my mother. He felt like he owed it to her at the very least. She was always so kind to him.
The knife slid easily through the moist brown chocolate cake. I sliced it neatly into twelve pieces. It was still warm in the centre as the knife moved through it.
The bell on the front door rang as someone entered the Café.
"Good morning, Sir. We won't be a moment." I heard Frank call.
He popped his head around the corner of the steel archway

to the front of the cafe.
"Can you please come serve this gentleman out front? I'll finish up in here for you." Frank was grinning smugly as he made his way into the bleakly clean kitchen. I lifted my eyebrows in confusion and headed out to the front, passing the knife as I went, the slim blade dangling from my fingers.
There he was. Smiling happily down at the menu in front of him. His black hair flopping smoothly over his pale face.
"Sorry." I broke his gaze from the yellowed paper menu taped to the white bench. His bright blue eyes met mine. My heartbeat soared within; my breathing suddenly hard to control.
"You're all good." He spoke. His deep voice was as smooth as honey. My heart patted gently against my ribcage.
"What can I get for you today?" I stood in front of him making sure to keep his gaze. Why was I so infatuated with this strange man?
"Just a large latte with one sugar today please." He looked at the menu down on the stone counter again.
I felt Frank move next to me. He placed the cake stand right by my arm. I could feel him watching me. His beady gaze burning into my flesh. I shifted uncomfortably.
"Not a problem. That will be four dollars fifty. Now was that to take away or to have here?" my voice shook.
"I think I'll have it here again today." He smiled his perfect lopsided smile at me. His blue eyes reflecting his happy smile.
"I will bring it straight over to you when it's ready." I smiled small, feeling Frank's continued gaze burn on me as I moved to the machine.
As I began to make the coffee, a wave of anxiety washed over me. I shot a cold sharp look at Frank as he brushed the already clean bench clean beside me.

A deep chuckle left his throat as he noticed it. He moved to clean the food display fridge that had been marked by people pointing at the item they wanted. Fingerprints on glass had always bothered me.
I was nervous. My heart pounded against my ribcage harshly and my breath caught in my throat. I began to feel shaky all over, as if my feet would fall out from under me. A cold sweat beading on my forehead.
I watched as he sat at a smaller table by the window and gazed out at the town. He looked peaceful as he observed the town people walking past.
I took a deep breath and continued brewing the coffee.

He flashed his brilliant smile once again at me as I walked over with his perfectly white and straight teeth. My cheeks flushed warmly. I walked in time to the soft cheery song on the radio. His eyes flittered back to a young woman outside. My shred of confidence seemed to disappear.
"Here you go." I chirped, breaking his concentration on the outer world and the girl in it.
"Thank you. I don't think I got your name properly yesterday." his blue eyes met mine again. My face grew hotter.
"Marty." I exhaled, relieved he didn't remember that it was Martha.
"Marty?" he questioned with a smirk.
"Short for Martha." I admitted hastily, wishing he had actually remembered it from yesterday, so I didn't have to repeat it anytime soon. My heart began to sink with self-doubt. As if he would remember someone like me. I am a literal nobody.
"Well Marty, I'm Eric. Eric Stone." He reached out a pale hand to me. I shook it softly. His smooth skin was warm on my cold hands.
"Lovely to meet you, Eric" a wave a confidence washed over me "What brings you down this way?" I asked, trying my hardest to act bubbly.
"Just wanted a breath of fresh air…" he was cut off by

Greg thundering in through the door.
"Just my today usual Frankie old boy!" he yelled. Taking his regular seat by the window. The bright light of the sun reflecting off the clean surface. I chuckled at his vigour.
"Coming right up, Greg!" Frank called from behind the grey marbled counter. His eyes rolling to the ceiling.
Greg took off his fraying brown woollen hat and observed the area as he threw it down on the table. His fingers tapping to the Fleetwood Mac song playing softly from the speakers. His gaze found me standing near Eric.
"Good morning, precious!" he grinned over at me.
"Good morning, Greg. How are you going this morning?" I turned my body and my attention away from Eric to face him.
"I feel like I want something sweet. You got the goods?" his tone cheeky as he raised a hand to his face to cover his mouth from Frank.
"I got the goods" I whispered, winking at him.
"That's my girl!" he punched the air excitedly. A laugh left my mouth at the gesture. I shook my head as I continued to laugh.
I headed back to the front counter and placed a piece of fresh moist cake onto a light blue plate for him. The chocolate cake slid easily from the knife onto the blue dish. Frank hummed happily to himself whilst he prepared the coffee.
Eric's focus was purely on his phone. A soft sigh of relief left my chest quietly. I waited patiently for the coffee.
I made my way over to Greg who watched hungrily as I sat his coffee and cake down in front of him.
"Thank you, my little love!" he exclaimed, picking up the small fork from the plate. I laughed to myself at his excitement. It was so sweet to see him so happy.
 "You are welcome, my dear friend " I replied with a grin.
"How much do I owe you for that?"
"For you, Greg. Nothing at all."
"Now you really are a saint, Marty Green!" he chirped.

He shovelled a big chunk of the chocolate mess into his mouth. The thick icing painted his white moustache brown as he devoured the dessert.

"This is really lovely, Marty. Now. Come here" he waved a hand at me gesturing to come closer.

I leaned over the dark metal chair that stood between the two of us and brought my ear close to his mouth.

"Is that your boyfriend?" he whispered loudly.

"No, Greg!" I jumped back. Making sure Eric wasn't paying attention. The sudden movement had gotten his attention, but it quickly went back to the phone in his hand.

"What?" he chuckled after wiping his mouth. I laughed at the thought of Eric even considering dating me.

"There will never be another man for me, Greg." I blew him a kiss. He reached up to grab it and as he caught it, he patted his heart. I could always have a joke with Greg. Greg's wife died three years ago so I made it my personal mission to bring even a little bit of joy to his day. He was always so sweet to me. He came off as an old uptight grumpy man who was stuck up but once you got to know him, he was truly the biggest sweetheart. He lived just four houses down from me and would always wave if he saw me pass in the mornings. Sometimes he would drive down and bring me some dinner he had made. Dad would always hide as Greg brought it over and we would sit and eat together, grateful for the simple company of each other. Greg loved cooking. His wife always used to cook with him until she got too ill to leave the bed. He cooked every single meal for her and always made sure to eat with her. He only ever talked positively about his wife. Never negative. Their tale really was a true love story. It was something I could only ever dream of having.

"Oh, my young love. One day you will meet someone who will sweep you right off those little feet of yours and away from this damned hell hole." He waved down at my small black work shoes.

"Maybe one day, Greg." My eyes wandered over to Eric

who was still staring absentmindedly at his phone.

The rest of my shift passed quickly as people poured into the café for their lunches and afternoon coffee's. The sun shone through the clouds overhead as I crossed the road to head over to my second shift of the day.
The supermarket stood in the centre of the town and had been there for years. The building was grey and dirty on the outside and weathered from the years of rain falling. The inside was just as bleak and underwhelming as the front.
The fluorescent lighting bounced off the dirty linoleum floors as I made my way to the dim staff room out the back. The usual day staff had left for the day and the night staff were ready to go home before they had even started. I hung up my bag and made my way back to the front of the small store to my register. None of the night staff talked to me unless they had to which I deeply appreciated. They were all friends from childhood who knew each other since day one. I was pulled out of school after my mother died to be home schooled by my aunt and uncle to avoid people altogether. They all assumed I was too broken or mentally unwell to be in school. Even before mum's accident, I was horrible at making friends. I had always preferred to be alone.
The shift began and I served anyone who came through, making small talk with them all as they passed through the checkout. Time passed quickly and I could not wait to be home. My stomach felt like it was eating itself with hunger. I had only eaten a bagel for lunch because it was much too busy at the café to take a full break.
"You sure are a busy girl, Marty." A deep voice broke my focus on my painful hunger. I looked up from the till and saw him standing there, smiling his lopsided smile with his blue eyes blazing. My heart race quickened. The pain in my stomach dissolving into butterflies.
"Well, I have to pay my bills somehow." I shrugged. He

chuckled softly. Shaking his head, his black hair flowing with the motion. My heart raced. His laugh was intoxicating. I smiled small.

"So, where else do you work?" he questioned me as I scanned a tin of diced tomatoes.

"Just here and the café." I responded.

"Do you do anything in your free time? That is if you even have any." he laughed. I felt myself smiling at his laugh, as if nothing more beautiful had ever graced my ears.

"Not really" I admitted "I like to stay home and read. I am not a very exciting person."

"Well, maybe you can show me around the town one day?" he asked cheerfully, his eyebrows raised questioningly.

My heart leapt to my throat. No one had ever wanted to do anything with me. Would I finally have a friend? A real friend?

"That sounds like a great idea." I smiled shyly, warmth spreading across my cheeks. The smell of his spiced cologne tingled my nose.

"What's your number? We can organise a time for when you aren't working." My heart leapt further up my throat as he spoke.

"Ahh…" I stuttered as I wrote my number on the back of a scrap receipt paper shakily. What was I doing giving a stranger my number? The pen jittered with my anxious hands.

I handed it to him along with his groceries as he tapped his card against the machine.

"May I talk to you later, Marty?" he asked politely.

"Of course, you can, Eric." I said softly. More heat rose in my cheeks as I blushed furiously. I could only image how red my face was.

The girl across from me serving at the opposite register smiled to herself at our conversation. She pushed a stray strand of platinum blonde hair behind her ear as she served the next customer.

My chest felt like it was on fire. I had never felt this way before. I felt blissful but also so full of panic. How could I have given my number to him? I felt like such an idiot. I mulled over my hasty choice for the remainder of my shift.

The clock hit seven pm and I packed up my register for the night. I said a polite goodbye to the girls on break in the back room and headed out the front doors swiftly, careful to avoid more social interaction.
I put my keys in the door to unlock my car. My phone buzzed harshly in my pocket.
I knew exactly who it was, but I was scared to read it. Why did he want to talk to me?
The street was silent in the nights fall. Orange lights flickered above the street from the old streetlights as I clicked my seatbelt on. I brought up the courage to check my phone. It shook as I brought it up to my face to read.
*"Hey Marty. It's Eric. How was the rest of your shift?"*
it read. The bright glow blinding me in the darkness.
*"Hey Eric. Not too bad, I suppose. How was your night?"*
I responded, unsure of what else to say.
I turned the key and started the drive home. The slow and soothing music filled the car from the radio, and I sang along with it as the car drove slowly over the slick road. The rain drizzling down again.
The road home was barren from other vehicles. Trees swayed in the breeze. Shielding the farm fields beyond.
My phone flashed its light brightly in the dark, scaring me. I swerved to the left. I wasn't used to my phone going off whist I was driving. My heart pounded with the sudden shock of my swerve. A sharp gasp left my chest. The seatbelt stiffened with the sudden swerve, bruising my skin as I slammed my breaks on.
I stopped the car on the side of the road to compose myself. Panic was rife through my body.
Wind whistled from the outside, trees swaying harder in the breeze. Illuminated in the bright full moon.

My head fell to rest on the steering wheel as I tried to concentrate on my breathing. The thought of me having an accident and my dad finding out invaded my mind. He would be distraught. To have his wife and daughter die the exact same way would kill him.

Pale moonlight shone through the clouds above whilst the gentle breeze swayed the branches of the trees to dance in the night. Tears stung my eyes with my depleting panic. I took my time breathing until I was ready to begin driving again. The ignition started loudly in the silent night air and my car rolled forward and back onto the main road.

I continued to ignore the text until I pulled up in the driveway of my house. The tyres crunched over the wet gravel as the car rolled to the front of the house. The porch light was on which meant dad was still awake. I finally checked my phone. I wiped my eyes clear of any tears before giving in to the blue lit screen.

*"Pretty boring. If I'm honest. I don't have too much to do here yet. Are you free tomorrow night to do something? It's okay if you can't. I don't want to come off as pushy."*

God, he really was keen. I tried to conceal my excitement. It felt like I was going to scream with happiness.

My emotions were all over the place by this point.

*"Can I check my roster and get back to you?"* I replied, putting my phone back in my pocket. I knew very well I was free all tomorrow, but I didn't want to come off as too eager.

I could see dad watching me in the car from the large lounge windows, making sure I came in the house safely. I pulled a funny face for him and watched him leave the window to come to the front door.

"Your highness!" he called. His voice muffled by the wind.

"Hi, dad!" I called out of my open window. I opened my door and got out of the car. Dad's brown hair shone with yellow in the light of the porch.

"Well come on in! I made us a nice roast for dinner with lots of vegetables because I know you love them so much." He waved a strong hairy arm toward the door. I smiled and hurried toward him and the warm house. The trees whistling in the wind. The damp smell of rain loomed in the air.

When I made it to the door, he swung his arm over me. He pulled me close. The strong smell of his spiced cologne stung my nose. I crinkled my nose but bared the scent. I hugged him tightly back. The memory of my swerve resurfacing. I squeezed him tighter. He squeezed me back with nothing but love radiating from his gesture.

"How was your day?" he asked, helping me take my coat off.

"Pretty ordinary." I admitted. My phone buzzed softly in my pocket.

"Who is that messaging you?" he asked nervously, looking down to my where my phone was concealed.

"It's just Frank." I lied. I couldn't tell him who it really was. He would have a fit if he knew I was talking to a boy. Dad walked into the kitchen ahead of me "How is Frank going these days anyway?" he called out to me.

"He's doing pretty good. Same as always." I called back as I shrugged off my coat, throwing it over the wooden banister of the stairs. I hung up my bag on the coat hooks and put my keys in the bowl on the front table. The pink wildflowers I had picked only a few days ago looked like they were starting to droop sadly already.

"I'll change them tomorrow." I murmured to myself, rubbing the soft velvet petals in between my fingers.

"Soup's up!" dad cheerful sang out. I breathed out a small laugh at his tone. The tantalizing smell of the roast dinner awoke the deep hunger in my stomach. My belly grumbled loudly.

I walked into the kitchen and sat at the small wooden table, placing my phone next to my empty lace placemat. I clicked the message.

*"No Problems :)"*
*"I am free as far as I know at this point."* I responded quickly.

I put the phone face down so dad couldn't read it. I knew how much he didn't like people and I didn't want it to annoy him with the subject.

He hummed the whole way over to me as he danced over with my plate. I let out a small laugh at his exaggerated spin.

"Here you go, Smarty Marty." He grinned as he placed the dish in front of me. Dad always made the best roast meal. It was nice to eat something warm. It was especially cold tonight. Steam swirled from the pumpkin and potatoes he had placed on my pastel green plate.

Dad sat across from me and began eating his chicken.

My phone buzzed again loudly against the solid table.

"What does that man want?" dad said through a mouth full of vegetables. I shook my head and covered my mouth as I ate.

"He just wants to discuss a cake flavour." I quickly lied on the spot with food in my mouth.

"Weird man, he is. Always was." He responded with another mouthful in his.

I agreed, trying to deflect the conversation.

I shoved a hot roasted potato in my mouth. Burning it slightly. I took a sip out of the frosted glass of water next to my plate, waiting for dad to speak to me. The water tingling my singed mouth.

"Are you working tomorrow?"

"Nope, but I do have plans for tomorrow night." I let slip.

"With whom?" dads tone changed to a harsh one.

"Just aunt Marion and Uncle John." I spat out another lie. My stomach twisted in knots. I hated lying to my dad.

"Your bloody aunt Marion needs to stay away from you. She had enough time with you." He waved his sharp steak knife at me.

"They just care about me, dad." I sighed as I cut the gravy covered mess on my plate.

"I do not like that woman. Not even one little bit." He stabbed the meat on his plate loudly.

"I know, dad." I said, startled at the loud pang of metal on porcelain.

We ate the rest of our dinner talking about the garden and what dad wanted to do with the house. He had plans to build a big vegetable garden and renovating his little back porch for the summer.
He always looked so happy when he talked about the house. He smiled and waved his hands in various building gestures as he spoke. I listened intently. It always made me happy to hear dad talk about his grand plans for the future and the house.
After dinner was finished and the kitchen was clean, I went up to my room and had a shower. Letting the warm water rinse the day away with all my lies I had told to my father. I felt dirty whilst I cleaned myself from the guilt, wishing it would wash away with the water.
The lavender soap intoxicating my senses as I washed the coffee and supermarket smell from my skin.
The bed called to me as I walked back into my room. The silky white sheets comforting me whilst I slid into their cooling embrace.
I checked my phone to see what Eric had said.
*"Perfect! So what time am I picking you up?"*
I panicked. He couldn't come to the house! Dad would kill me!
*"How about I meet you in town?"* I suggested.
*"I am more than happy to pick you up."*
*"That's alright. I live a fair way out of town."*
Dad's heavy foot falls came up the stairs. I locked my phone quickly and slid it under my pillow.
A knock hit the wooden door softly.
"Come in, dad." I spoke loudly. He opened the door and looked in. My room was homey. Very warm and inviting. The same vibe I intended for the rest of the home to have. I had a bookcase full of books at the end of my large bed and a large window that looked out to the surrounding forest around us. I hardly ever closed the thick cream

curtains. Sometimes I would leave the lace ones closed but the majority of the time they were open as well. I enjoyed the way the moonlight shone its way through in at night when it wasn't raining and flooded the room with its peaceful, pale light. The moonlight would reflect off the faded pine wooden floorboards and the sunlight would dance on them.

I had a single set of fairy lights pinned above my wooden bed on the wall for an extra bit of ambiance. Mum always had them in her room. She said they looked like little stars here on earth.

"I just wanted to say goodnight." He made his way over to my bed against the window and leaned down to me. He kissed my forehead softly, his sharp stubble grazing my eyebrows. He ran a hand over my hair. "You are so much like your mother, kid." He said with his voice filled with sorrow.

"I know, dad." I could see the tears begin to brim in his deep blue eyes.

He said nothing but smiled and left the room. Closing my door behind him.

I sat up against the hard-wooden oak bedhead and clicked my phone awake.

*"So when and where then?"* his message read.

*"There's a bar at the corner of the main street. We could meet there at around eight?"* I suggested. I could stop in and see Marion tomorrow for dinner before I left that way. I usually went over there on a Friday for dinner anyway. A good clause to add to my ongoing lie.

*"Sounds perfect to me. I'll see you then."* He responded.

I stared out the window. The moonlight beamed out from behind the clouds. I wished mum was still here. She'd tell me what to do tomorrow. Was this even a date?

I pondered on my choice of outfits and how I could get away with being out so late. I would tell dad I was staying at Aunt Marion's after dinner to watch a movie. That could work.

I slid back onto my plush pillows. Thinking of my day ahead.

## Chapter Five

"Martha!" Dad yelled as he pounded on my hard door, rousing me from my deep sleep.
"What?" I groaned loudly.
"Come downstairs and get your breakfast!" he called, his voice getting softer as he made his way back down the stairs.
I rubbed my eyes before I opened them. The sun was shining from the window onto my bed. I smiled at it. It was rare to see the sun out so brightly in the morning.
I slid out of bed and stretched my stiff body. Some parts cracking as I moved for the first time in hours. I let out a long yawn and put on my fluffy blue dressing gown. My shoulders snuggled deeper into the comforting fabric.
My thick socks stifled the sound of my sleepy foot falls on the stairs. I slid my hand over the smooth pine banister as I made my way down. Dad was singing in the kitchen to himself. I couldn't help but smile.
He stood over the stove in his red flannel pyjamas and sang his heart out to an old grungy rock song on the radio. I observed him as he stirred the small pot of oats on the stove with his wooden spoon. Cinnamon lingered in the air.
"Good morning, kiddo!" he called, not taking his eyes off the pot.
"Morning, dad." I pulled my right leg underneath me as I sat at the round wooden table. A yawn escaping my mouth

whilst I settled in.
All the windows in the house were open letting the fresh autumn breeze fill the old house.
"How'd you sleep?" he asked.
"Fine. What about you?" I said through another yawn.
"Pretty well actually." Dad turned to the kettle on his right and poured the water into two deep mugs. Careful not to spill any boiling water on the counter.
He finished cooking the oats and transferred his clumpy creation between two white bowls. Pouring honey on mine and putting dark frozen berries on his. He placed the bowls down on each side of the table and our mugs of tea next to them. Dad would always make sure to have meals together when we could. It wasn't often we were both home from work in the morning. Even though Dad worked from home, I never really saw him during the day.
He shoved a mouthful of oats in his mouth and looked at me. "What are your plans for today?" he said through the food piled in his mouth.
I swallowed my mouthful and answered "I think I will go out to the field and pick some wildflowers for the hall. I might read for a bit or something. Then I'll head out in town to go to Marion's at about four and have dinner and watch a movie. What about you? What are you going to get up to?"
"I am going to work from my bed and then I might read one of those fantasy novels you always have your nose in and relax for the night." He waved his spoon at my nose. A smile crept across my face.
"Sounds very lovely dad." Dad was always interested in the books I read. Although he never really read them for himself.
"Make sure you look after your uncle John. He would be in absolute hell living with that woman." He pointed his spoon at the front door.
"I always do, Dad. You know that." I ate another spoonful of my warm clumpy oats.
"Good kid." He smiled proudly at me.

We finished our breakfast, and both went our separate ways.
I headed up the stairs to put on some old clothes to go down the field in whilst dad went to his room and closed the door.
I slid on a pair of dark red jeans that were old and stained with dirt from years of playing outside and an old shirt I stole from dad years ago. I brushed my thick hair and slid it back into a messy ponytail. The waves dancing as I hurriedly brushed my teeth before racing down the stairs. The sunshine reflecting off the red undertone of my hair making it look like fire blazed through it. Throwing the back door open, I raced for the field.

I loved going into the field just past our house, right on the edge of the forest. The wildflowers bloomed so vividly there. It was breath taking.
The flowers swayed in the soft cool breeze as I passed through. The pastel and earthy colours mixing beautifully together in a swirl of art. I ran my hands over the longer blossoms. The velvet petals soothing my hands. The scent was intoxicating. You could spend hours here and still be amazed by the multitude of colours amongst the greenery. My eyes wandered over all the flowers. Trying to decide which ones to pick were always hard. I settled for a mixture of the longer stem ones and headed back down the quiet path I had made from my years of travelling to and from into the house. My hands grazed the soft flowers around me. The sweet earthly scent getting more pronounced with each step I took.
Our house was the last on the street. No one ever had a reason to come down this far unless they wanted to go into the forest, which no one ever did.
As soon as I got home, I changed the flowers over. Feeling more at ease with a new set of fresh blooms in the crystal vase. Just the way mum used to.

I smiled to myself. The long hours spent in the field brightened my mood to a point where nothing could destroy the joy I felt.

Curling up on the couch with my tarnished novel in hand, I listened as dad shuffled his way through the house before delving into the story.

It was just after three in the afternoon when I finished my book. It was almost time to prepare myself for my fist date.

I didn't want to look like I was trying too hard, but I didn't want to look like a slob who didn't care at all.

Warm soapy water swirled down the drain as I stood in the shower, sing along to my favourite song playing from my phone.

The sweet tune swooning about wishing to be normal. The connection to the lyrics hitting a deep level of my soul.

"Maybe someday I'll be normal." I mumbled glumly to myself. The taps hot against my hands as I switched them off. My eyes shut tight to avoid the pain of leaving the showers distracting embrace.

Stepping out at last after becoming too cold with the lack of water, I wrapped the towel around myself. The rough and worn cotton rubbed harshly against my skin as I darted back into my room. My phone still playing the soft folk song as I threw it on to my bed, muffling the sound slightly.

Turning my attention to the wooden wardrobe in the corner. Soft flowers painted with oil paints dotted the front doors. A small pang hit my heart. Even here, I couldn't escape the longing for my mother.

The wardrobe itself was full of a multitude of different pieces I had collected over the years from various thrift shops but nothing nice to go out in as I was never invited to go anywhere.

I sorted through the dresses stuffed in the back corner out of sight. My hands grazed the one right at the back of the cupboard. The soft cotton soothing my shaking skin.

My mother's old floral navy-blue dress.

Mum used to wear this dress all the time. The memory of how captivating she looked in the dress overwhelmed me. It was like it was made to fit her body. She would always find an excuse to wear the piece whenever and wherever she could.

The urge to try it on overtook me. I slid it over my head. Pulling on the elbow lengths sleeves.

The dress fit like a glove, sliding easily over every small curve on my body. I glanced at my reflection in the mirror, the familiar sting of tears hit the back of my eyes.

My resemblance was too much like her. I couldn't bear to wear it out, but there was nothing else that would suffice on such late notice. Cursing myself for not going to the shops earlier, I flattened out the worn skirt and swivelled my hips to watch the dress circle me.

"Maybe I can make it a little more me." I said to myself, trying hard not to let my tears fall.

I moved over to my chest of drawers placed next to my wardrobe and pulled out some black stockings. I slid them on and added a pair of deep red boots I had gotten from another thrift store in town a while ago.

"Better." I nodded to myself whilst I slid on a thin silver belt.

The silver topped it off perfectly, complimenting the small yellow flowers beautifully.

I brushed out my hair and let it fall in a mess of natural waves, sliding on a black head band to keep the frizz from my face.

I never wore makeup but today brought the sudden urge to. I had only ever done the basics so that's what I went with. I swiped on some mascara and concealed my dark under eyes before using my finger to tap on some pale champagne shimmery eyeshadow Marion gave me a long while ago. I slid a shimmery lip gloss brush against my lips. The sickly-sweet peach flavour was enough to make me wretch. The cold gel shone in the afternoon's dimly fading light.

I felt like a whole new woman as I stared at my reflection in the mirror. I didn't even recognize myself. The person staring back looked new and full of life. Someone whole. Someone who wasn't me.

Was this even a date? Was I putting in too much effort? The panic had begun to set in. my heart raced in my chest. My hands rattled by my side. A sheen of sweat glistened above my brow.

The clock on my phone read 3:50PM. Time to head into town.

"Bye, Dad." I called as I raced out of the house, carefully avoiding his gaze. Knowing he would question my outfit if it was only for dinner.

"Bye, baby! Stay safe!" he called back. His booming voice muffled by the closing of the door. My heart pounded in my ears as I shut the front door behind me. The warm autumn sun spreading its light over the forest was captivating to look at. If I had more time I would have gone for a walk through the brush.

The key clicked in the ignition. The roar of the engine erupting in the still night. It was now or never.

## Chapter Six

"Look at you!" Marion's cheerful voice cooed as I walked hastily up the front steps of her white porch. Aunt Marion stood with arms wide open for me. Her blue eyes glistening with happiness. I hugged her small frame. Her jet-black hair bun hitting my nose as I embraced her. Her olive skin glistening in the afternoon sun
"I thought I would make an effort for dinner this week." I shrugged.
"Well, I am certainly glad you did" she looked me up and down "John! Doesn't Marty look absolutely lovely this evening." She called out to the warm house behind her.
"Most beautiful girl I have ever known." John materialized behind Marion.
"Thanks, Uncle John." I smiled up at him. John was a good foot taller than Aunt Marion and looked the total opposite with this bright orange hair and soft brown eyes.
"I got something cool to show you, kid." He reached past Marion to grab my hand. I followed him through the elegant house I had grown up in and out the back to his shed, or 'workshop' as he preferred to call it. John was a builder by trade but had always loved carving wood. It was his personal outlet.
He opened the steel doors to the shed and held it open for me. I stepped into the dim shed. A light flicked on overhead, brightening the room. The smell of wood heavy in the musky air.

The room was full of pieces that Uncle John had spent hours meticulously carving. There were so many beautiful intricate pieces in the shed such as a statue of a goddess, a fish and an older style bookcase.

The piece I had always found so beautiful was an oak crib that John had carved for his first born. He had poured his entire soul into the oak crib. He had carved stars all along the side and moons along the rails. I could feel Uncle John's pain every time he looked at the crib, radiating in the dust filled air. It was never used. They had tried for years to have their own children and suffered many heartaches along the way. But still they ended up stronger for it and ended up raising me. Guilt bubbled in the pit of my stomach. I had always felt unworthy of their love. A part of me still did now.

"Here it is." John interrupted my thoughts, his tone cheerful despite him standing near the crib.

"What is it?" I asked moving over to his dirty work bench covered in a mess of assorted wood shavings. Dust swirled in the ray of light that shone from the window.

John placed down two dark book ends on the table. They were beautiful. He had smoothed them down and even carved in little flowers in the shape of a heart. I reached out for them. The dark wood felt as smooth as silk under my fingers.

"I love them!" I breathed out. They had taken my breath away. My cheeks burned with the extent of my smile.

"I was out here alone and missing you around bugging me like you always used to so I thought I would make you something." He looked so pleased with himself but so sad at the same time. A mix of emotion I had grown used to.

"Thank you so much, Uncle John." I hugged him tightly, the smelt of spices and pine curled in my nose with comfort. He hugged me tightly back as if he never wanted to let go.

"I'm glad you like them, kid." He nuzzled his head into the crown of my head.

"I love them!"

"I love you." He breathed.
"I love you too, Uncle John." I squeezed him tighter.
"Let's head in before your aunt gets mad." He groaned slightly as he straightened up after letting me go.
"We really don't want that." I laughed, breaking the tender embrace.
"No, we most certainly do not." he chuckled as we made our way up the stoned garden path back to the house.

"Wash your hands!" Marion yelled from beyond in the living room the moment we stepped through the back room.
"Always something." John grumbled deeply to himself as he slid his boots off at the back door. I bit back a laugh as I washed my hands in the laundry sink.
"And wipe your feet also!" she called back.
I rolled my eyes and followed John inside to the kitchen.
"Spaghetti for dinner, Smarty Marty." John pointed to the pot on the stove. I loved Aunt Marion's spaghetti. I would sit and eat serving after serving of the meal until I was sick when I was twelve. Marion had no choice but to put me on a ban until I was sixteen.
"My favourite!" I bubbled. My stomach awoke with a small rumble.
"We saw you were a bit down at Whybourn's café yesterday when we walked past so we thought we would cheer you up tonight with your favourite meal." Marion said as she entered the room. She stood out like a sore thumb amongst the pure white kitchen. Marion was very clean and particular when it came to her house. Nothing was ever out of place, and nothing was ever dirty. She could spend hours a day cleaning and still not be satisfied in the slightest.
"Thank you, Marion." My heart ached at the thought of someone going out of their way just to see me smile.
"Anything for you, kid." Why was everyone calling me kid so often now.
"I'm twenty-two!" I laughed.

"And?" John questioned with his eyebrows raised.

I smiled and shook my head, letting it go.

"John, can you please go and set the table." Marion pointed to the next room with a wooden spoon.

"Yes, dear." He sighed. His footfalls becoming softer as he left us alone in the kitchen.

Marion bent her neck to watch him go down the long hallway.

"He misses you terribly, Marty. He was in your old room the other night 'fixing it up'" she used her fingers to do quotation marks.

"I'm sorry I don't come over more often." I sat up on the bench. Guilt clouded my mind.

"Martha, get off my bench!" Marion hit my leg softly with the wooden spoon she had just cleaned, and I hopped off the counter only to lean against it. Marion rolled her eyes dramatically. I pouted at her. She said nothing.

"You have your own life! Don't worry about us oldies." She smiled and pinched my cheek with her perfectly manicured nails. I snarled at the gesture.

I pulled my face away and she laughed. I hated when she did that. My cool hand soothed where she had pinched me.

"Your mother used to where an old dress just like that one." Her blue eyes looked me up and down.

"This is mum's old dress." I picked up the skirt and smoothed it out.

"You look an awful lot better in it than your mother did."

"Thanks, Maz." I giggled.

"Martha. Do not call me that! Go and help your uncle set up for dinner." She barked. Another spoon to the leg. Her sneer softening at my laugh.

I made my way down the white hall and into the dining room. Marion loved her dining room. It was her 'pride and joy' as she called it.

"Need some help?" I asked John. He jumped back in shock, almost dropping the expensive plates on the red carpeted floor.

"Jesus Christ, Marty. You scared the day lights out of me."

He breathed heavily whilst placing the clean dinner plates on the white clothed table. John leant against the chair closest to him, his hand clutching his chest.

"Sorry!" I shrugged. The plates were always the same. White with gold leaf over them. They were very elegant. We used them every Friday I was here. I was grateful for everything they had done for me but a part of me felt horrible for seeing them because I knew the pain it had caused dad. They raised me when Dad couldn't, and I know he hated them for it. Even if he wouldn't admit it. We set the table together and discussed how work was going for both of us. John's work colleague had quit to help take care of his newborn son and John had been doing his workload for him as well as his own. He never stopped. He would work until his hands bled. The only time he ever took a sick day was to hang around with me when I was feeling down. He would work with the worst cold and sickness and would power through any and all heartbreak. The strongest man I knew.

"So, Marty, how have you been?" he asked, putting his plate down at his spot to the left of Marion's spot at the head of the table.

"I've been really well actually." I admitted cheerfully.

"That is actually fantastic to hear, Martin!" he smiled at me over the table.

"Thank you. How about you, Uncle John. Are you doing well?" I asked looking him in the eye.

"I'm good. Just working hard. Day in, day out." he shrugged limply.

"I hope you aren't lying to me again." I pressed. My brows raised.

"I'm not kid. Trust me." He smiled. Uncle John would always hide his feelings from everyone. It was as if he didn't want burden anyone with his issues.

"Good." I nodded.

The table was set for dinner as Aunt Marion came in. She placed the big pot of pasta down, looking pleased with herself.

"Smells lovely, my dear." John licked his lips hungrily at the large pot on centre of the table. The rich aroma pooling saliva in my mouth. My tongue darted over my lips with excitement,
"Thank you, my love." She smiled and kissed lightly him on the cheek.
Marion took her seat at the head of the table as always and ordered us to eat.

As we ate, Marion spoke of her week. She whined about her job constantly. She was a teacher at the local high school. She said every year the kids were getting worse and worse.
"They just do not listen at all!" Marion exclaimed from the lip of her wine glass.
"Thank god we home schooled you then, Marty." John said with a mouthful of pasta.
"Yeah, thank god." I agreed. Marion shot him a scathing look for talking with his mouth full.
"Sorry dear." He muttered into his hand to hide his mouthful.
When I was younger, John was my teacher. He would teach me every night after work, and he would come home and teach me until dinner was ready. He would make sure to finish at three pm every single day to ensure he was here in time to school me. After, Aunt Marion would teach me for a night session until about seven pm and then it was time to wind down for bed. I was so grateful for the amount they had altered their lives just for me.
The golden clock on the white wall read 7:30. It was almost time to meet Eric. A sharp lump rose in my throat. The cutlery in my hands beginning to shake. My leg bounced under the dinner table. My stomach began to churn with nerves, my dinner threatening to come back up with the thought of it.
"I need to be somewhere at eight." I announced as I took a sip of my iced water.

"You got a date?" John asked jokingly. Marion choked on her deep red wine.
"Not a date exactly. We are just friends." I shrugged, trying to keep my cool. Anxiety crept through my body. Marion patted her mouth on her napkin, careful not to smudge her deep berry lipstick.
"Look out, Marion! She's on the prowl!" John raised his hands to look like claws.
"I am not!" I laughed and threw my cream-coloured napkin over at him.
"So, who is he?" Marion asked over the rim of her wine glass. Her beady eyes narrowed on me.
"A new guy in town. He mentioned he didn't know anyone here yet so I said I would show him around." I looked down at my empty plate, stained from the spaghetti. Marion sat grinning at me over her glass. A rush of hot warmth filled my cheeks.
"I am so happy for you, Marty! Our little girl is growing up, John!" she cheered to him, shaking her fists with vigorous enthusiasm.
"Thank you, Marion. But we are honestly just friends. I barely know him." I tried to make my point clearer, pleading with my eyes.
"It's great to see you have a friend, kid." John was smiling at me too.
I guess me being a loner was weird to them after all. My heart began to sink deeper in my chest.
"I better go." I pointed at the clock with a frown.
"Yes! We can't keep you from your date!" Marion cheered, clapping her small hands together.
"Please stop calling it that." I begged, rising from the table.
"Alright, smarty Marty." John laughed.
"Thank you." I poked my tongue out at him. He followed suit and poked his out too.
"You are more than welcome." He chuckled.
"You two are so weird." Marion shook her head at us. Her black bun bobbing in the motion.

I wished dad was able to come out. I knew he never would though. He hated Marion. He didn't leave the house at all. He was unknown to everyone. And I was harbouring his dirty secret. My skin felt dirty at the thought.
I removed the thought from my head and looked at John.
"Well, go on then! Go to your hot date!" he ushered me to the front door through the living room.
"Oh my god! It's not even a date. I shouldn't have said anything to either of you." I groaned. John let out a deep laugh at my response. Marion chuckled along with him. We walked to the front door. The cold wind blew through me as John opened it wide, sending shivers down my spine. My skin rose with goosebumps.
"Did you bring a coat?" Marion asked from behind me. I wrapped my arms around myself in a bid to keep warm.
"I forgot." I frowned. How could I forget my coat in this town?
"I'll go get you one." She left to go back into the house. She emerged a few seconds later with a navy blazer.
"Here." She handed me the suede coat. It was elegant for what it was, and it suited my outfit well. The gold button glinted in the porch light.
"Thank you." I kissed her cheek and hugged uncle John before heading to my car.
I reversed out of the drive and the tug of nerves pulled sharply at my stomach. I glanced as they stood waving. John had his arm over Marion's shoulder. He kissed her head as she waved. A loving smile filled her face. I wished I knew what it felt like to be loved by someone that deeply.
"Here goes nothing." I mumbled, turning the key in the ignition.

## Chapter Seven

The only parking spot out the front was behind a flashy new silver sports car.
"What kind of idiot would drive that here?" I muttered to myself as I reapplied my clear lip gloss, pulling the stray hairs out that had stuck to it.
I smacked my lips as I looked at myself in the rear-view mirror.
"Not too bad." I said to myself proudly as I admired my appearance.
I slipped my small black leather cross body bag over my shoulder and took a deep breath. My mind was racing as I reached for the door handle. What was I even doing here?
The cold breeze carried me into the old corner building.
The bar was almost empty when I walked in. I could feel myself shaking as I looked around the near empty room for Eric.
There he was. Tall and handsome in his dark blue suit. Leaning against the bar with his beer in hand talking to the bald bar keep. My stomach tied itself in knots and I froze. Struggling to take a single step forward any further. I was panicking hard. My hands gripped the strap of the body bag hard enough to make my knuckles blanch white.
Eric turned in my direction and spotted me the moment I had pushed to fully open the heavy metal door. His eyes raking over my trembling form.
He grinned a wide smile, waving me over. I shakily put

one foot in front of the other and made my way over to where he sat against the bar. A shy smile plastered on my face.

The bar keep nodded at me but didn't say anything. He moved away from the two of us to another customer who had walked in behind me.

The bar was small and dimly lit but Eric's smile illumined the whole room. The sporting memorabilia giving it the standard pub feeling. The scent of alcohol was rife in the damp air.

"How have you been?" he said happily, grabbing my forearm gently.

"Well." I breathed, still out of breath from my panic at the door. His touch sent tingles through my arm. Butterflies fluttered in my stomach as I looked into his baby blue eyes.

"Good to hear. This is actually quite a nice little bar." He pointed out. His head swivelling to look over the building. I looked around and nodded. The deep oak furniture gave it more of a rustic look against the red walls and carpet.

"It's not too bad." I noted.

I had never actually been in the bar. The smell of yeast tainted the cool air. Why didn't they have the heater on in here?

"So, what did you get up to today? Anything fun?" Eric sat on a tall stool behind him.

"I went into the field by house and picked some flowers and then I went inside to read a book. I had dinner with my aunt and uncle then came here" I shrugged "not an overly exciting day. What about you?"

"I worked all day." He took a sip of his amber beer.

"What do you do for work, Eric?" I asked. I fumbled for the barstool behind me as I sat down to face him. My nerves slowly fading, I breathed in deeply, trying to gather my confidence to continue talking. The scent of his woody cologne tingling my nose.

"I am an accountant." He smiled.

"Oh, really?" I tilted my head.

"Yeah. I got sick of living in the city" he took another sip from his beer glass. The bubbling liquid sliding into his mouth.

"Why would you come to a town like this? It's always so gloomy down this way." I asked, raising an eyebrow in confusion. No one ever just came here.

"I like the gloomy things. The saddest things are sometimes the most beautiful." He admitted whilst looking directly into my eyes.

"Fair enough." I mumbled, feeling uncomfortable in his gaze for a slight moment. I shuffled my hands on my skirt uncomfortably.

"Where are my manners?" he laughed again "Would you like a drink?"

"That's okay. I'm driving." The uncomfortable feeling faded with the sight his smile.

"You can have at least one with me." He pressed; his brows raised with persuasion.

"Sure, I guess." I gave in to his allure.

The bar keep came back and poured us both a beer each. I never really like alcohol, but I suppose I had never really given it a chance before either. It was a night of firsts for me. I smiled to myself proudly. Eric smiled at the sight of me brightening. It took all I had not to grin like a lovesick fool.

We spoke for an hour about little nothings and just got to know each other. I learnt his favourite colour was green, the same as mine and that he loved to cook.

I was open with Eric about myself. He was the only person I felt I could be truly open to. He had an aura of peace around him, and I felt safe when I was near him despite the incredibly short while I had known him.

Eric raised the beer glass to his plump rosy lips and guzzled the last tiny amount of the beveridge. Following suit, I hurriedly finished mine as well. The fizz coating my throat. It felt like I was drinking static. A dry bitter static.

"Would you like to show me around town now, Marty?" he asked cheerfully.

"Of course, Eric." I looked at the antique clock on the wall, it was nine pm.
Nothing was open in town this late at night, but I could still show him around the small main street.
We headed out from the cosy bar into the cold street. Eric's phone started ringing loudly from within his coat pocket. I shoved my hands in the blazers pocket to keep warm in the frosty air. My breath fogged as I exhaled sharply. I hopped from foot to foot to stay warm.
"Excuse me." He reached for his phone and answered it. The call becoming urgent as he tried to calm the other person on the line down. He hung up the phone and ran his hands through his thick dark hair.
"I am so sorry, Marty but I'm going to have to head home. My housemate is freaking out over something stupid."
"That's okay, Eric. No stress at all." I reassured him with a smile. I dug my hands deeper into the pockets for warmth.
"I had good night" he smiled shyly "Would you like to continue this some other time?"
"Of course." I imitated his shy tone, regretting so after seeing the look of panic on his face.
Eric nodded at me and headed for the silver sports car. A hearty laugh escaped me as he opened the door.
"What?" he heard me laugh and spun around to face me from his door.
"No one in this town drives a car like that." I giggled, pointing my key to his car.
"Well, no one in this century drives a car like that anymore." He pointed at my red truck.
"There is absolutely nothing wrong with my car." I called to him defensively.
"It's the twenty first century, Marty." he called back, laughing to himself.
"Goodnight Eric." I called as I got in my car. The windows had fogged in the cold night air. I put the key in the ignition quickly
The engine rumbled to life as I turned the key. Eric was already gone and speeding down the road.

I drove home buzzing that night and not just from the alcohol.

## Chapter Eight

I woke to the sunshine blazing into my eyes. Another sunny day. My tired hands rubbed the sleep from my eyes and sat up. There was no noise coming from downstairs like there usually was on a Saturday. Where was dad? My fingers glided over the wooden banister of the stairwell. The wildflowers scent filing the small room. A smile creeped happily across my face at the smell of them. I made my slow way into the kitchen only to spot a note on the table.

*"Marty, I have to leave for a while. No time to explain but I won't be back for a fairly long time. I have left you money in the drawer in the hall table and some food in the freezer. Stay safe. I love you always. - Dad."*

I put the note down sighing, he seemed to be leaving more frequently these days. He used to leave every now and again with no explanation but these days he seemed to be gone more. I always felt so alone when he was gone.

I felt a sadness take over me as I prepared my cup of tea. My phone buzzed violently from within my robes plush pocket.

The screen illuminated with a message from my boss at the supermarket. I had lost my job. They had cut back all night staff. No thank you for your efforts just letting us know the change was immediate.

This day could not get any worse.

I didn't respond to the message. I just left it on read. A part of me was relieved that I didn't have to go there for work anymore, but I was sad for the loss of money. I didn't do a lot that involved money anyway, although I did spend a fair amount on books each month.

The couch was soft and inviting as I sat down on it. I sipped my tea whilst I watched the sunshine spread in the forest surrounding the empty space across the road. It brought me peace to look at the insects and wildlife flying around the flowers and plants as they swayed in the breeze. I curled my knees up and balanced my cup between them as I smiled at the outside world.
My phone buzzed loudly next to me. My peaceful bliss shattered with the sudden noise, causing me to jump with fright. The teacup teetered on my knees.
My hands fumbled as I read the message.
*"Hey, Marty! I am so sorry for leaving early last night! I feel so bad for leaving as I did. What are you up to today?"* the message from Eric read.
My heart leapt to life in my chest. I grinned to myself. Warmth spread across my cheeks.
*"Hey! That's okay, Eric. I was really tired anyway. I am not up too much today at all. What about you?"* I responded.
My phone buzzed again not too long after. The teacup shaking in my hands as I raised to my lips.
*"Nothing, I was wondering. Because I desperately need to get out of this house, and I love to cook. Would you like me to bring over dinner and we could watch a movie together?"* he asked.
My finger fumbled the teacup as I read the message, a splash of hot tea fell onto my pyjama bottoms with the sudden movement. Dad wasn't home at the moment, so that wasn't an issue, but I had never had a boy come over before or anyone else for that matter. What would they even want to do here?
*"If you really want to you can."* I sent nervously. I

bounced my legs up and down with nerves. The teacup now placed on the level ground away from my nervous form.

*"Awesome! Are you allergic to anything? Or dislike anything?"* he asked.

*"Whatever you cook will be fine. I'm easy to please."*

*"Cool. What's your address?"* he asked.

"*23 Kingsley way. It's the last house on the road."* I responded.

*"No worries, I'll be there by say six? Is that alright?"*

*"Sounds good to me."*

My mind was racing. I had so much to do before he came over. I had to clean and straighten the house. It was clean enough for my standards, but I still had to neaten it before Eric came over. I hurried upstairs and threw my robe onto my bed. There was no time to waste.

I vacuumed the house and mopped the pale wooden floors. I cleaned the dishes left in the sink from dad's dinner yesterday and ran a cloth over the dining table. I fluffed each cushion on the couch and straightened the blankets dad had put over them.

My feet scurried up the stairs to the shower. My finger raced as I scrubbed my scalp vigorously. The scent of the lavender shampoo helping to calm my growing anxiety. Dressing in a pair of plain black jeans and a light floral flared sleeve top, I felt more at ease as the time began to pass.

"Everything will be fine." I assured myself as I looked at my frantic face in the mirror.

I made my bed and smoothed over the smooth white bedding. I picked up the clothes off the floor, throwing them in the washer and then hung them out on the clothesline to dry them outside in the warm sun.

I finally sat down just after four pm. What was I going to do with my time?

Deciding to read to fill in the time before Eric arrived, I sat down in Dad's white armchair and extended the footrest.

A cold breeze filling the room as the clouds hid the sun. The scent of dad bringing me the comfort I craved, as if he were here to hold me and sooth my worries.

I decided to light the wood fire in the loungeroom to warm the slowly cooling house and sat down in front of it to keep myself warm whilst I read, just like I did when dad wasn't here sometimes. He couldn't tell me off for using too much power. I turned the lights on the wall on and continued reading.

The crunch of gravel outside tore my attention away from the novel. My body trembled with anticipation.

Eric's silver sports car pulled up next to my red truck looking tiny compared to it.

He got out of the car with grace and walked to the passenger side door where he grabbed a green fabric bag and bottle of wine. I swallowed hard as I watched him walk to the door from behind the lace curtain.

I stood shakily by the window and waited for the doorbell to ring, hoping he hadn't seen me staring. He rang and I answered slowly.

He grinned at me as I let him in to my home. His white teeth shining in the dim porch light.

"Welcome." I greeted him.

"This is a beautiful home, Marty." he looked around as he slid his brown leather shoes off.

"Thank you. Here, let me help you with that." I offered, reaching down and taking the heavy bag from him and headed into the bright kitchen.

"Do you own this place?" he asked, admiring my home. His gaze wandering over everything he could see. I only hoped I hadn't missed a spot in my cleaning rampage.

"I do. Well, my father does." I shrugged. My eyes widened as a realised what I had said.

"Is he here?" Eric asked cheerfully, looking around the kitchen.

"No. He isn't here." I needed to change the subject "So what's for dinner?"

"I made us a homemade curry." He announced proudly.

"Oh." I was shocked. I sat the bag down on the table in the centre of the room.

"Don't you like curry?" he asked, disappointment tainting his tone.

"No" I said with panic. "I have just never had it before, that's all."

"You've never had a curry?" he asked, clearly taken aback.

"Nope."

"How have you never had a curry!" he exclaimed in shock. His brows raised. The blue of his eyes glistening in the setting sun.

"Just never have I guess." I shrugged, feeling insecure. I wrapped my hands around my waist to comfort myself. Circling my thumbs around my biceps.

"Well, I hope you like this one. It's just Butter Chicken." He pulled the orange sauce container from the bag. Still warm from the stove he cooked it on.

"I'm sure I will" I tried to persuade myself.

I pulled two deep yellow bowls from the cupboard next to the stove and sat them next to his containers on the table.

"You look lovely tonight, Marty." he said softly as I stood next to him. I blushed furiously. The heat spreading to the tips of my ears. My arm softly grazing his.

"You do too, Eric." He was wearing blue jeans with a grey casual shirt that fit him like a dream.

He dished up the curry into the two bowls, clearly pleased with himself.

"It smells amazing." I noted. The spicy aroma filling my nose with excitement. Saliva pooled in my mouth with the sheer thought of tasting the meal.

"It'll taste just as good hopefully." He waved a spoon at me as I sat across from him in dad's usual chair.

"I know it will." I smiled small at him, trying to hide my excitement.

Eric placed the large bowl in front of me. The spiced scent intriguing my senses. I had always eaten quite plain and basic foods as that's what everyone else had cooked for me. But I was always eager to try new things. I just needed the confidence to do it, that was all.

I watched as Eric put a spoonful in his mouth and I followed suit.

The curry was heavenly. The chicken was tender, and the rice was fluffy. It was instantly a favourite of mine. My mouth watered for more with each mouthful I took.

"This is amazing." I looked at Eric with my eyes wide with excitement.

"Why, thank you. I am glad you like it" Eric said proudly. He grinned over at me as I ate his meal.

We ate our dinner in silence before heading into the living room.

My heart leapt out of my chest as I looked around the room to make sure it was clean enough.

Eric walked over to the mantlepiece above the roaring fire, observing the pictures in the frames with interest.

"Is that you?" he laughed, pointing at a small gold framed picture.

I walked up and joined him, his arm grazing mine once again. Heat rose from the place his skin touched me. He was looking at picture of me when I was wearing mum's wedding dress playing dress up.

"Yeah. I was eight when my father took that." I felt a sad pang in my heart.

"Who is this?" he moved onto the next photo. It was my favourite photo of my mother. She was in her wedding dress in the field next door laying amongst the wildflowers.

"That's my mother, Maree." I exhaled. I knew the topic would come up sooner rather than later.

"She's beautiful." He noted.

"She was the most beautiful person I'd ever known." I hugged myself for comfort.

"You look just like her, you know." He looked from the

picture to me and back again to the picture. I had always been told me how I do look just like her. Each time hearing it, it me with as much sadness as the last.
"She was the sweetest soul. She cared so much about everyone around her more than herself. I miss her more and more every passing day." I admitted softly
"Sounds just like you too. Where is she now?" he asked, looking around the house.
My breath caught in my throat and a familiar sting of tears hit my eyes. I wouldn't cry yet though. I would wait until after he left, and I was once again alone with my secrets.
"She passed away when I was eleven." I looked down at my feet to avoid his gaze. I nibbled at my bottom lip.
"Oh, Marty. I am so sorry to hear that." He apologised, raising a hand to my arm gently.
I moved from him and sat on the couch, patting the empty cushion next to me as a gesture for him to sit and join me. I held a pale-yellow pillow close to my chest for comfort. The cotton soft under my tired fingers.
"It's alright, Eric. I'm okay." I smiled. "It was a long time ago now."
"May I ask how it happened?" he held my hand in his. A harsh lump forced its way into my throat.
I breathed in and considered what telling him everything would do. It all fell out with the slightest of ease.
"My mum and dad weren't happy being together anymore." I divulged.
"Oh" he breathed.
"Mum was planning to leave my father for another man and take me with her or something, I'm not too sure of the exact reason. I was dad's reason for living and he wasn't going to let me go. Mum went out one night to go to the store during a storm to get me some supplies for a school project we were working on. Dad was up in his room all night working so I sat at the front window and waited for her to come home. She hadn't been gone very long when a police car came up the driveway. The police asked to

speak to dad, and he broke down in front of me. He went insane with grief. Rumours circulated the town that my father killed her, and I guess he couldn't cope with it, so he fled. He left me here alone."

"So, who raised you, Marty?" Eric was aghast.

"My Aunt Marion and her husband John. Marion was mum's sister. She took me in and schooled me from home and raised me into who I am today. Uncle John looked after the house for me so that when I turned eighteen I had somewhere nice to live." I shrugged sadly.

"Have you spoken to your father since?" he looked me in the eyes.

"Of course." I said without realising what I had said until it was out.

"So, you know where he is?"

"No" I lied "He didn't tell me. It was only once. It was nice to hear from him." I tried to dispel the thought of my father being around. The familiar dirty feeling rose over my skin.

"I'm so sorry to hear that you went through all of that, Marty." he said softly and took both of my hands in his, squeezing them tightly.

"I'm alright, Eric. Honestly, it was a long time ago and I know she is always here with me now." I squeezed his hands I return.

"You are truly the strongest person I have ever met." He leaned in closer to me. I smiled up at him.

"I just pushed through, I guess." I scrunched up my nose as I smiled.

His face inched closer to mine and I felt myself leaning forward for him. My heart racing as my lips were centimetres from his. I closed my eyes, awaiting the embrace. His lips touched mine softly. The taste of wine tinged my mouth. Sparks erupted in my body as he reached a hand up and cupped the back of my head. He pulled himself away from me just as quickly as he had kissed me.

"I am so sorry, Marty. I don't know what came over me."

He looked at my lips hungrily.

"It's okay, Eric. I quite enjoyed it." I grinned stupidly at him. A warm blush flooded across my body.

I finally had my first kiss.

Eric smiled warmly whilst moving his gaze to my eyes. My body felt electric as the butterflies fluttered in my stomach.

"Shall we watch a movie?" he changed the subject. Wiping his palms on his jeans.

"Sure." I was nervous. What if he didn't mean to kiss me? Regret ran through me.

We put the movie on, and he put his arm around me drawing me closer to him. A sense of calm radiated from his body to mine. One secret I'd held was finally off my chest and I felt amazing.

## Chapter Nine

I woke up the next day feeling amazing. My body felt as if it were full of happy butterflies, and nothing could ruin my mood. I danced out of bed and sang in my morning shower. I never sang in the shower. Eric was bringing out a side to me even I had never known.

My phone buzzed softly from my room.

*"We should go out to eat tonight."* Eric wrote.

*"Where did you have in mind?"* I asked.

*"How about that pizza place three doors down from the café?"* He suggested.

*"I have never been there. But sure! I'm keen for anything."*

*"I will pick you up at six."*

*"I'll meet you there."*

*"No. I will be picking you up. End of story. :)"*

*"Alright. Fine. I'll see you then."* I gave in.

I had never been in anyone else's car but John or Marion's beside my own. A slight rush of nerves flowed through my body.

I looked at the clock. I had slept until twelve in the afternoon. The mix of emotions form the night before drained me.

I opened the back door and headed down my path into my field.

My body relaxed as I lay down amongst the blooms. They curled to my skin in the slight autumn breeze. The sun

peaked through the clouds above at me.
"Hi, Mum." I said to the sky. "I've missed you so much lately. Well, more than usual." My shoulders slumped.
A tree branch in the distance waved gracefully in the soft wind. A breathy laugh left my chest. My mind felt at ease as the tiny purple flowers blossomed around me in the midday sun. Their sweet earthy smell lingering on my body. A familiar feeling of happiness greeted me once again.
Time passed quickly as I wandered through the field looking for blooms. It was hard to decide which ones to pick. They all looked gorgeous to me. I wandered to the edge of the forest. The greenery thick from the latest storm.
I checked my phone. Five pm.
What had I been doing for the last 5 hours!
I rushed inside and practically flew up the stairs. I didn't have time to have another shower. I didn't even know what I was going to wear.
My hands searched franticly through my wardrobe. Landing on a plain black dress in the back.
"That'll have to do" I mumbled.
I slid on the thick dress and tugged at the high neckline. The sleeves tight against my arms. It was almost a size too small, but I didn't have much else. Looking in the mirror at myself, I styled my hair into a neat bun on the top of my head and applied my minimal makeup. Feeling slightly more at ease.
My silver jewellery box on my chest of draws glinted in the light, catching my attention. I walked over to it cautiously. The lid creaked as I opened it. It was full of mum's old jewellery.
One particular piece stood out amongst the rest.
The silver lotus necklace. It was small and dainty, but it still had its alluring shine.
Dad brought it for my mother for her twenty first birthday and then he had regifted it to me for mine. I had never

worn it though. One day I hoped to pass it along to my own children if I were to ever have any.

A knock at the front door downstairs startled me. I dropped the small necklace on the ground in my fright. "Coming!" I called as I scooped up the necklace. It was a fight to get it on as I hurried down the stairs, mumbling various curses in my frustration. My fingers fumbled against the latch behind my neck. I tripped over my own feet on the last step and fumbled to the floor with a thud. "Ouch." I groaned as I rubbed where my hip had hit the banister. The necklace finally done up as I sat on the floor, wincing with the sharp pain.

I opened the heavy door to find Eric standing there smiling. A bunch of pink roses stood out against his black attire.

"Marty. Are you okay?" he asked. His eyes lingering on where I was holding my hip with caution.

"Yeah, I'm fine." I assured him with a smile, trying my best to steady my breathing. A hand waving away his concern.

"I brought these for you." He handed the bunch of roses over to me, taking my word.

"They're beautiful!" I breathed in shock. A grin crept across my face. My cheeks warmed with blush. I kept my hand on my hip for comfort of the sharp pain I had stupidly given myself.

"You look beautiful." Eric looked me over. His eyes lingering on where I was holding myself again with worry.

"You look pretty good yourself." I chuckled.

"We look like we are about to go to a funeral." He noted, laughing at himself. He too was dressed all in black.

"I can change if you want." I hoisted a thumb over my shoulder.

"No, you look great." He laughed and pulled me outside. I put the roses on the entry table and followed him to his silver sports car.

"Did you fall over before you answered the door?" Eric asked, concerned about my stature.

"What makes you say that?" I tried to laugh it off.
"I heard a loud thud, and you groan something."
"I had hoped you didn't hear that." I sighed with embarrassment. Eric laughed softly.
"Are you okay, Marty?" he asked, brows furrowed.
"Yeah, I'm just very clumsy." I flashed a warm smile at him.
I had to lower myself to get into the vehicle. The scent of a sweet air freshener tingled my nose as I sat on the cold leather seats.
I shuddered at the cold on my bare legs.
"Are you cold?" Eric asked as he sat down.
"The seats are freezing." I cringed.
"I'll turn the heater on." He reached for a knob on the dash.
"The heater is on." I pointed at the illuminated heater button.
"The seat heater." He laughed.
"What! They are actually real?" I gasped "I thought they were only in movies!" my eyes wide with wonder.
Eric let out a long hearty laugh.
"Have you been living under a rock, Marty?"
"No, my car just doesn't have them, Eric." I jutted.
"I'm surprised that old thing even has a heater." He joked.
I shook my head and stuck my tongue out playfully at him.
"That car is older than both of us and runs one hundred times better than anything I have ever been in before." I defended my car.
"My god." Eric laughed deeply again.
"What?"
"You're so funny, Marty." he chuckled. I shook my head and looked out at the starry night sky. I smiled to myself. Thinking of mum watching down on me. She would have loved to see me laugh with a boy. I wish he could have met her. They would have adored each other.
He shifted gears and the engine roared to life as he put his foot on the pedal. The noise vibrating through my body.

My hands automatically reaching for the door to hold on to for support. Or dear life. I wasn't sure which.
Eric laughed again when he saw me tightly dripping his door.
"I'll drive nice and safe for you. Don't worry." He reached over and put a hand on my thigh.
"Thank you." I managed to breathe out. Panic flooded my body at his warm touch. The spot he grazed cooled instantly when he placed his hand back on the wheel. The delicious heat from the seat heater curled against my bare legs. How could I have forgotten stockings in this weather! The sports car was much smoother than my old car. It rolled graciously over the road as if it owned it. Eric hummed along to an old rock song playing over the car's stereo. It sounded like an old one dad used to listen. The name escaping my mind with the twinge of loneliness I felt in dad's absence.
We rode in silence until Eric pulled up out the front of the local Italian pizza restaurant.
The old brick building was lit up and full of inviting light.
"Hold on. Stay right there." Eric said as he got out of the door.
I sat still and waited to see what he was doing. My pulse thundering in my ears as he walked behind the car and around to my door.
"My lady." He bowed as he opened it. His pale hand extended for me to grab. I giggled at the gesture.
I smiled as I took it. His skin was warm in the crisp night air.
Eric's hand continued to hold mine gently as we made our way into the bright restaurant.
"Welcome." The waiter greeted us as we walked in. He stood tall over the small plastic partition he was stationed at. His deep skin shining in the yellow lights from above. The lime green walls clashed violently with the grey floor beneath us. I pulled my hand from Eric's and held both of my own together for comfort, but he was quick to claim it back.

The smell of tomato and fresh herbs filled the air with soft piano music playing softly in the background. It was a whole new experience for me. My eyes grew wide with wonder

"Just a table for two please." Eric raised our hands. An uncomfortable feeling curled over my spine with the waiter's gaze on our hands.

"Right this way, please." He led us to a table in the centre of the room. I sat down and waited for Eric to follow suit. I looked behind him. A table of girls I had worked with at the supermarket stared at us in sheer disbelief. My heart dropped down to my stomach. I was kidding myself that Eric actually liked me in anyway apart from a friend. The sudden anxiety had taken over my mind. The blissful peace I felt shattered in an instant.

"This is nice." Eric broke my thoughts. I turned my gaze to him from my lap where I had glumly lowered it to. His beautiful ocean eyes blazing happily at me as if he didn't see my sudden change in character. My heart leapt to life again.

Behind him, one of the girls had gotten up from her table and was approaching us. Her long icy blonde hair trailing behind her slim stature.

"Martha!" she bent down to hug me as she arrived. I went rigid with fear as she wrapped her slim arms around me, stiffening at her friendly touch.

"Hello?" I squeaked with anxiety. I had forgotten her name, but she had always been kind to me whilst we worked at the supermarket. I recognised her as the one who had smiled when she spotted Eric talking to me in the supermarket.

"It's lovely to see you out and about for once! We never see you out anywhere but the little café." She spoke. Her voice sweet like honey.

"I don't really have a reason to go out." I shrugged. Looking at Eric for any kind of support. He watched on with a smile on his face, clearly not thinking anything of the situation.

"Well, now we all have another one. Were you let go of at the Supermarket too?" she tapped her pink manicured nails on the wooden table.

"Yes." I admitted, looking at her deep hazel eyes.

"Us too." She pointed to the other girls who all waved.

I nodded at them and avoided their gaze.

"Where are my manners!" she exclaimed "I'm Charlotte!" she reached a bronzed hand out to Eric.

"Eric." He shook it slowly. His gaze drifted to her slim face, and they locked eyes. My fists baled in my lap. They were more suited for each other. Maybe the kiss was an accident last night. My leg bounced with nerves beneath the table.

"You must be new around here." She noted. Her tone becoming flirty.

"Yeah, I just moved here from the city actually." He shrugged a thin shoulder

"Luckily Martha got her claws into you before anyone else could." She laughed, pushing my shoulder jokingly.

"Well, she sure is one hell of a girl." Eric laughed back. His stare turning to me. I looked down into my lap. My nails had dug deep crescents into the fleshy skin of my palms.

A rush of unnerving anxiety ran over me. I had never even spoken two words to Charlotte. Why was she here making such a fuss?

"Oh, I bet she is." She looked over me happily. I turned in on myself.

"Mmhmm." Eric hummed whilst keeping his happy smile plastered in his face.

"Excuse me." I stood shakily and hurried toward the bathroom. The grey tiled floors clicking under my shoes. The door screeched as I opened it. It was all too much.

I looked at myself in the mirror. My pale skin had blanched with fear. Bile rose in my throat, and I tried to keep it down. I rested my hands either side of the basin to collect myself. When I finally looked at myself in the mirror, I had blanched as white as a ghost.

"You're fine." I assured myself, repeating until I began to feel better. I took a deep breath and headed back to the table. Eric and Charlotte were both laughing happily as approached the table.

"Well, I better get back to the girls." She clapped her slim hands together in front of her lap as I made my way back to the table.

"It was lovely to meet you, Charlotte." Eric smiled up at her.

"And you, Eric. Martha, now we have some more free time maybe you would like to come out with us for a drink or dinner one night soon. We would love to get to know you more! We just hate seeing you so alone all the time." She turned to me, flashing a pearly white grin.

My heart raced with more nerves. I sat down slowly to steady myself. My trembling fingers gripped the chair beneath me.

"That sounds good. Thank you." Was all I could manage to say. She seemed genuine but I wasn't too sure. I smiled small, silently cursing the fact that my crippling shyness ruined everything.

"You're welcome. What's your number, Marth? Maybe we can organise a girl's night sometime soon?" she asked.

My mind raced again, and the bile threatened to come back up.

"Sure." I gave her my number shyly. She smiled and waltzed of to her table. Her long blonde hair flowing behind her like a curtain of silk. The other girls at the table gave me a smile and a wave as I glanced over at them.

"She seemed nice." Eric said as he took a sip of cold water from his glass on the red wood table.

"Yeah, she is I guess." I mumbled.

"Are you alright?" he asked nervously.

"Yeah, of course. Just needed to use the bathroom." I lied and waved it off. Eric frowned but took my answer as the truth.

The waiter came over to give us a menu and take our drink order. Eric ordered a glass of wine for us each. The waiter left to get our drinks quickly. I took in a harsh breath as I read the fancy black leather-bound menu. My eyes rolled over all the enticing options. All new and exciting. I struggled to pick just one. I didn't like seafood at the best of times, but I was willing to try anything.
"What are you thinking?" Eric asked. His blue eyes sticking out from behind the menu.
"I'm not sure yet." I admitted.
"Too many options."
"Way too many." I chewed my lip.
"Pizza?" he asked, wiggling his eyebrows.
"I'm thinking maybe a pasta." I nodded.
"Oh, good idea."
I glanced over the menu again for the pasta section.
My eyes read over every option. Lingering on the pumpkin risotto.
"I'm going to have seafood." Eric announced. I winced at the thought of the dish. The stench it would radiate. I hated seafood more than anything.
"Very nice." I lied. "I was thinking of getting the pumpkin risotto."
"Have you ever eaten it?" Eric jokingly asked.
"Nope." I noted.
"Good choice then." He took a swig of the bubbling white wine that the waiter had sat down.
"I think so." I grinned proudly.
The waiter came back and took our order. I watched him as he left to head back toward the kitchen area.
I felt Eric's stare burning into me. His eyes drinking in every millimetre of my face.
"What are you looking at? Is there something on my face" I asked anxiously. I took a sip of wine to calm myself.
"You truly are a beautiful woman, Martha Green." He said without ever moving his eyes from me.
I felt a large goofy smile grow across my face. Blood rushed to my cheeks, burning as it spread.

"Thank you, Eric. You are pretty good looking yourself." I winked at him.

Eric let out a deep hearty laugh.

"Thank you." He grinned. His cheeks flushing with a rosy tint.

"How's work been?" I asked to change the subject. I shifted awkwardly in my seat

"Work is work." He shrugged and took another sip of wine. Following suit, I took a small sip of mine. The white liquid sour against my tongue, trying my best to hide the disgust.

"That's good?" I questioned.

"I'm still adjusting to the smallness of this town." He rubbed his neck slowly.

"It's peaceful here." I smiled.

"It's too peaceful. Everyone seems so content here. Don't get me wrong, it's a good thing but just very strange."

"Well, we are an awful lot smaller than the city, Eric." I took another sip of the dry wine. I didn't like it much. I screwed my face with obvious disgust this time.

"That's for sure." He grunted, finishing his wine. He gestured for the waiter and ordered a different kind of wine. A crisp and bubbly golden liquid flooded into the glass. I was grateful. The waiter left just as quick as he arrived.

"Is that a bad thing?" I questioned him, cocking my head to the side.

"No. Not at all. I just want to explore. There is so much world out there, Marty. So much unseen wonder. I want to see as much and do as much as I can." He said excitedly, his bright blue eyes shining with amazement of his own dream. I silently wondered what it's like to have such a grand dream.

"If you wanted to explore, then why come here?" I asked.

"I needed to get out of the city. I had issues with an ex-girlfriend." He shrugged off my question.

"Right." I nodded. Would he think I'm a loser because I've never had an ex-partner?

"You can come with me!" Eric suggested excitedly.
"What?" I laughed, taken aback by his suggestion.
"You can come travel with me! We can visit Rome or France or anywhere you want to go!" he cheered. His eyes smiled at me happily. My heart raced at the sight. "I hear Rome has some of the best ancient libraries in the world."
"Eric, I would love to, but I can't. I have my family here and my house and job. I can't just pick up and leave." The truth was I could easily up and leave if I wanted to, but the fear of my father would always hold me back.
"Come on, Marty. It'll be fun! It won't be forever." he grabbed my hand in his over the small table. A rush of electricity ran through my hands. My mind raced at the thought of running away with him. That was a grand dream to be had.
"Okay." I submitted. It did sound really fun and exciting. I had always wanted to visit other places in the world, but I didn't think I ever could.
"This is going to be great! Have you ever been overseas?" he asked excitedly.
"No. I haven't even left this town." I laughed sadly. I sounded pathetic.
"You've never even been to the city?" he narrowed his eyebrows with sheer disbelief.
"No, not yet at least." I answered. My fingers fumbled for the stem of the wine glass as nerves took over my body. I swigged down the contents of the glass. My eyes watered from the fizzing bubbles as it slid down my throat.
"Can I offer you another glass, ma'am?" the waiter approached the table.
"Please." I nodded, my anxiety churning in my stomach. He poured the same bubbly liquid into the glass, and I took a swig the moment he left, hoping the alcohol would wash down my nerves.
"You're so very peculiar, Marty." Eric sat observing me.
"Thank you?" I responded confused. My eyebrow cocked with the motion.
"It's not a bad thing." He assured me.

"Oh, that's good then." I raised the glass to lips for another sip.

"I actually find it very attractive." He spoke. I spat my mouthful back into the glass with shock. The fizzy bubbles flooded into my nose painfully.

"Shit." I mumbled under my breath at myself.

"What?" Eric chuckled at me, sliding me napkin over the table. I picked it up and wiped my face. The smell of wine staining my skin.

"I don't think being peculiar is very attractive." I said, my voice hoarse from chocking.

"Well, I think you are attractive. And you are peculiar. So, there for peculiar equals attractive." He gestured as if the two words were coming together. I rolled my eyes.

"I am not attractive, Eric. That girl that came over before" I nodded at the table of girls eating their pizza "*She* is attractive. Not me."

"I beg to differ."

I let out a snort and Eric smiled at me and shook his head. His thick black hair swaying in the motion.

"Let's agree to disagree." I suggested.

Eric nodded and sipped his wine.

The waiter placed our food on the table. The sheer scent of Eric's seafood made me feel queasy. The smell of fish had always made me feel ill, so I had never tasted it. I looked down into my own dish. The thick orange rice smelt divine. The steam wafted off the dish, carrying the creamy aroma of the food straight into my nose. I took a small mouthful hesitantly.

The rice was hot in my mouth. The sweet taste of the rice mixed with the creaminess of the pumpkin and the bitterness of the cheese ignited my senses. I had never eaten something so plain yet so delicious. My eyes lit up in wonder. How have I never eaten something wonderful like this before!

"Good?" Eric asked after swallowing his mouthful.

"So good." I marvelled at the dish. My eyes were wide with delight. My tastebuds exploding with the rush of something new touching them.
Eric laughed at my uncontained excitement over my dinner.
"How is yours?" I asked.
"Not bad." He shrugged, still smiling at my reaction.
"It doesn't look bad." I leaned forward to look closer at the dish. A small prawn poking out through the white sauce turned my stomach. I quickly turned back to my meal.
"Would you like to try?" he offered.
"I've never eaten seafood. So not really but thank you for the offer."
"How? What were you raised on?" Eric said, visibly shocked by my response.
"Mum used to cook a lot of vegetable meals and Marion eats very clean, so it was usually a lot of basic foods, unless Uncle John was cooking. He made some amazing meals. Have you heard of a chicken parmigiana?" I asked.
Eric let out a deep hearty laugh.
"Wait, are you being serious?" Eric looked me in the eye as he read my confused face.
"Yes?" I furrowed my brows.
"Oh my god!" Eric burst out in an echoingly deep laugh. The table of girls looked over at us confused by the sudden outburst.
"Shut up, Eric! It's not funny!" I laughed at him.
"How have you never heard of a parmigiana?" he laughed loudly once again.
"Stop it!" I laughed along with him.
"You are too pure, Marty." he took a deep breath and continued to eat to calm himself. His eyes shone with glee as he continued to smile.
I practically inhaled the food on my plate. The warm dish bringing me comfort with every mouthful. We finished off the bottle of wine between the two of us, with me devouring more than him.

We ate our food happily before making our way up to the counter. I pleaded with Eric to let me pay for my half of the cheque but to no avail. He wanted to be a gentleman, so I finally gave in and let him. The happiness from a good meal and the buzz from the alcohol had me feeling amazing as if I was as free as a bird and as light as a feather.

"We should get you home." Eric said as we stepped outside of the restaurant.

"Yours or mine?" I joked. I was shocked at my own confidence. The alcohol began to take its toll. I extended my hand to him. My mind bubbled with happiness.

"Well in that case Ms Green…" Eric took my hand and led me to his silver sports car laughing.

"My lady." He opened the door for me. I laughed at his valour. My body gliding gracefully into the car.

"So, where are we going?" I asked as he slid himself into the car.

"Let's go to your place. It's quieter." He nodded, pressing a button on his side of the dash.

"Sounds perfect to me." I purred, wondering who I was turning into.

Eric's sports car rumbled to life. The soft purr of the engine filling the quiet night air.

The road home was full of laughs as Eric tried to sing along to a punk rock song playing on his stereo. His voice going higher with every line of the song. Even though it was out of tune, I still found it beautiful. He laughed at himself. I could feel myself falling in love with him more and more every time he laughed. It was the most beautiful thing I had ever heard. My heart felt full.

We pulled up the dark driveway of my house. The porch motion light turning on with the movement of the car. Eric got out of his drivers' seat and walked back around to me. He opened the door once again, his pale hand extended out for me to take.

I placed my cold hand atop his warm one gently. I stood from the car and fixed my skirt.

An arm slid behind my back and another behind my knees as Eric bent down. He hoisted me up into a hold. I wrapped my arms around him with joy, giggling relentlessly at the fact that he was carrying me to my house.
"What are you doing?" I burst out laughing.
"Let's get you inside." He whispered into my ear.
"Why are you carrying me?" I laughed.
"Shh." He ushered as he carried me to the door. He turned the handle, and the door flew open.
"I thought I locked that!" I giggled at myself.
"Naughty!" Eric said as he tossed me lightly onto the couch. I laughed loudly at his efforts.
"I am not *naughty*. You are the one who distracted me!" I shouted after him as he shut the door. Eric cracked a joke about me falling for him and it took all my strength not to admit that I was.
The moon light poured in from the large front window. The trees swayed lightly in the breeze beyond.
Eric went to the small control panel on the wall and turned on the heater. I laid still and watched his movements. He moved so gracefully with each step unknowingly. His beauty oozing out of him as he flicked on a floor lamp near the fireplace.
Eric turned to me laying on the couch admiring him.
"My god." He exhaled. His chest heaving in the motion as if he was breathless.
"What?" I panicked and moved my hands to my face. I touched it lightly to see if I had food stained on my skin.
"You are just so beautiful, Marty." Eric moved closer to me. His eyes hungrily looking into mine. My heartbeat hard against my chest as I sat myself up.
"I'm really not Eric…" he cut me off with a swift kiss. His smooth lips were soft against mine. Gentle at first than harder with fiery passion. My hands snaked up his strong arms and nested at the back of his neck. His soft black hair cool against my fingers.

He moved his body closer to me so that he was practically on top of me. I began to feel myself panicking. I ushered myself to concentrate on nothing but him. It worked.

My body was alive with passion. All I wanted was Eric. All I needed was Eric.

Eric's hand moved up to cup my face and I nuzzled into it. His soft hand moved from my face down to my shoulder and I moaned with excitement. Eric pulled away from me slowly.

"Sorry." He breathed out heavily. His chest rising and falling harshly.

"For what?" I asked.

"I couldn't control myself." He panted.

"It's alright, Eric. I don't mind. I rather enjoyed it." I assured him.

"You just amaze me." he grinned his lopsided grin at me.

"And you amaze me." I reflected his smile.

## Chapter Ten

"Marty!" Frank called from the front of the café.
"What?" I called back.
"Your lover boy is here!" He sang out.
"Oh, will you just shut up about that, Frank!" I whined.
I walked out the front just in time to see Eric walk in the door.
He gave me a goofy grin when he spotted me at the counter. His blank gaze giving away the fact he didn't hear what Frank had said. A slow exhale left me with relief. My stomach churned with butterflies as I stepped toward the counter.
I had seen Eric every night for the last two weeks. Each night I seemed to get a little closer to him. Seeing him was now my favourite part of my day. He came into the cafe every morning I was rostered on just to see me before his day at work started. I could feel myself falling more in love with him every time he so much as looked at me. His blazing blue eyes could melt me anytime they looked directly into mine. His calming energy always drawing a thick blanket of comfort over my skin. I had really gotten to know him better than I had ever known anyone before, and he knew me better than even Aunt Marion. I only ever wanted him.
"We still on for that movie later?" he asked as I handed him his tall takeaway coffee cup, latte with one sugar, just as he always liked.

"Yours or mine?" I asked. Looking into his misty eyes.
"Yours." He purred as he took the paper cup and ran his palm over my hand that now shook with an onset of nerves.
"Sounds good to me." I fumbled on my words; my breath caught heavily in my chest.
He smiled and left the store. My heart raced after him. The sun poured in from the windows outside, dancing on his hair as he ventured for his car.
Frank came to my side with the biggest grin I'd ever seen him sport around me. The expression causing my brow to quirk
"He really is a lovely boy, Marty." Frank assured me.
"Thank you, Frank." I turned away from him smiling.
"Ahh, and here comes your aunt." Frank pointed to the door with a huff.
Marion walked in. Her deep black hair up in a high bun with a brown suede coat covering her pure white shirt underneath.
"I saw that, Marty!" she gushed. Hurrying to the counter with her high heels clicking on the plastic lined floor.
"Saw what?" I played dumb, getting a stiff roll of the eyes in return.
"You know exactly what I saw! You should invite him over for dinner sometime!" she begged. Her browns eyes pleading with me. A sheen of excitement radiating her features.
"I can't, Maz." I shook my head and picked up a cloth, avoiding her gaze as I wiped my counter.
"Why not! It's Friday!" she whined. I had completely forgotten what day it was. What was I going to say to her! I couldn't say no.
"How about you come over home for dinner and you can meet him then?" I suggested, immediately regretting my choice.
"Perfect. It is my night off anyway! I'll get John to drive so we can have a little wine together! Oh, I'm so excited!" she raised her hands up like an excited little kid.

"Marion, please…" I whined.
"My little baby is growing up!" she cut me off before I could finish my plea.
"Fine. I'll see you at six." I shook my head again and began wiping down the already clean counter. Marion's grin spread from ear to ear.
Marion left the store quickly and was straight on the phone. No doubt telling John all about tonight.
I pulled my phone out of apron pocket and fumbled a quick text to Eric.
*"Change of plans…"*

\*\*\*

It was four in the afternoon when I had gotten home, and I could feel a storm coming over head.
The wind blew harshly around me as I left the comfort of my warm car. The steel of the car door slamming loudly in the hard gust.
 A white slip tacked to the front door caught my attention.
*"Marty, I came home to grab some things but I'm going to be gone just a bit longer. I love you."*
Dad's handwriting scrawled a mess on the already wrinkled paper.
I unlocked the door and headed inside. Cold air hung heavy through the home. Throwing my keys in the dish by the door, my gaze turned to the crystal vase. The flowers I had picked only days ago now wilting, I took them gingerly out and ventured back out into the gale to pick fresh ones. A bunch of purple sweet peas had sprouted in the east corner of the field and that's what I had picked. The sweet scent stronger with the brewing storm.

Once inside with the wildflowers placed back into their home, I started to prepare dinner. I wasn't a good cook like Eric was, but I was still rather proud of the meal I had made.

Marion's old spaghetti recipe never failed. I cooked the sauce and left it on the stove to keep warm before heading up stairs and showering the endlessly bitter scent of coffee off my skin.

As I made my way back downstairs, thinking of what needed to be tidied, a knock on the door startled me. I opened it cautiously. No one was meant to arrive yet.

Uncle John stood beaming at me from behind the fly wire.

"You guys are early." I looked at the clock. It was only five thirty. The door creaked as I pushed it open for them.

"Your crazy Aunt Marion would not wait a single second longer than she absolutely had to." He rolled his eyes and nodded his head back at her.

She was walking quickly up from her small white car with a cake in her hands.

"I brought dessert!" she wiggled her hips as she sang. I hadn't seen her this happy in a long time. It was nice to see her smile. My own lips curled at the sight.

"Thank you, Maz!" I moved to let them through to the kitchen. She huffed at the nickname I had called her but didn't say anything further.

I hunched over the stove, boiling the pot for the pasta. The hot steam warming my cold skin. I silently prayed for the heater to kick in and warm up the house.

"So, when is this boy getting here?" John scoffed.

"John! Don't say that about Martin's boyfriend." She smacked him on the chest playfully. He chuckled in return.

"He is not my boyfriend." I turned away from them. I wished he was. I pouted to myself.

"He is a boy, and he is your friend" she gestured two things joining with her hand's "boyfriend" she spoke proudly.

"Thanks for that explanation, Einstein." I snorted at her. A warm blush flooded my cheeks. I turned back to the pasta to avoid her gaze.

"Oh, Martin! It's going to be a great night!" she sighed happily, ignoring my retort.

"She had a very tall glass of wine before we left." John pointed his thumb at her.

I laughed as she smiled up at him. They were always so happy together. It was a lovely sight to see.

A knock on the door startled me as I drained the boiling pasta.

I put the pot down on the sink and wiped my hands on the front of my clean grey pants.

"Coming!" I called as I hurried down the hall. Marion whispered something to John, but I was too far away to hear exactly what it was.

My fingers fumbled for the doorhandle. I was scared to open it. I turned the knob gently. How was I still nervous after all this time?

There he stood. Smiling at me with his blue ocean eyes. A black woollen sweater pulled over his standard blue pressed work shirt.

"Hey, Marty." he leaned in and kissed me on the cheek.

My eyes drifted closed at the exchange. A sense of longing overcame me.

"Hello." I was breathless at the sight of him.

"Can we talk later?" he asked seriously.

"Sure, is everything okay?" I said worriedly, shutting the door as he stepped through.

"Yeah, I just need to talk to you about something." He smiled at me. His gaze drifting to the kitchen.

"Alright." I mumbled. A wave of anxiety washed over me, replacing my longing with fear.

I lead him through to where Marion and John stood waiting.

"Hello, Eric!" Marion cheered whilst she pulled him in for a tight hug. He towered over her short stature.

"Hello." He said back happily as he hugged her.

"I'm Marion and this here is John." She waved at where John had perched leaning on the bench near the stove.
"How are you, mate?" John reached out for his hand.
"I'm good, how about yourself?" he shook John's hand back. Anxious nerves coursed through his deep voice.
"Not too bad." John said. John eyed Eric over but gave a small warm smile.
John approved. I breathed a thick sigh of relief.
I watched silently as Eric sat down at the table and began to converse cheerfully with Marion and John, his nerves seemingly faded.
"So, Eric, what do you do for work?" John asked him.
"I am an accountant." Eric answered happily.
"Good. You are a smart man then I presume?"
"I like to think so." Eric shrugged whilst holding his perfect white smile.
I shot Uncle John a warning look. He changed the subject immediately, shifting awkwardly in his chair.
"Are you the one that drives that silver sports car around town?"
"Yes, That's my pride and joy." He admitted proudly.
"I have always been curious about those cars." John scratched at his clean-shaven chin.
"Would you like to come see it?" Eric offered and pointed toward the front door.
"Sure, mind showing me the engine?" John stood and followed Eric to the door.
Marion leaned back in her chair to watch them leave. Craning her neck for the second they shut the door.
"My god! He is just so handsome, Marty!" she noted loudly.
"Very." I nodded in agreeance. The sense of longing washing back over my skin, wanting only to follow Eric outside.
"And a smart boy too." She took a sip of the red wine poured in front of her.
"Yes, he is." I blushed.

"Do you *like* him?" Marion looked at me with questioning eyes.
I looked out the window to where he and John were talking. John had his head under the bonnet of Eric's car. A sincere smile plastered on Eric's face.
"I really do." I admitted aloud.
"I knew it" Marion stood "Your mother used to look like just like that at your father when they first met. Of course, she didn't like him much in the end but no matter." She waved a perfectly manicured hand in front of her face as if to wave the memory away. She stood and silently moved to where I was gazing out at the boys from the archway to the lounge.
Marion grabbed my shoulders from behind and perched her head lightly on my left one.
"I miss your mother more and more with every passing day, Marty." she sighed. Her head nuzzling into the crook of my neck.
"Me too, Marion." I reached up and patted her hand, not taking my gaze. off Eric. Tears pricked behind my eyes.
"She would be so proud of you, sweetheart. You do know that, right?" her voice turning watery.
"I know. Thank you, Aunt Marion." I nestled into her embrace. A sad smile filled my face. I would have loved for Eric to have met my mother. An empty piece of me growing in my chest.
"And you so know that I am always here for you and that I love you so much. You remind me so much of her." Her warm lips kissed my temple softly.
"I love you too." I closed my eyes and enjoyed her hug.
My eyes flew open at the sound of the front door clicking open. The boys came in talking of cars and various other motor vehicles. Marion took her seat back at the table quickly. My hands extended in front of me to take hers. She gripped them tightly. A fresh sheen of tears crossed her eyes.

"You didn't tell me that your old car was your mothers!" Eric said to me suddenly, breaking the tender moment I held with Marion.

"I didn't think it was necessary." I quirked a brow, looking confusedly at Marion. She looked just as confused as me. Her thin eyebrows furrowed. Her hands drifted from mine back to her wine glass.

"I meant that I thought you just brought a truck because you like old things." He tried to explain himself. His face flushed with embarrassment.

"Oh, right." I drawled, still confused by the outburst. Eric was obviously more nervous around Marion than John than I thought.

"Marty's mother Maree used to drive that car everywhere. She used to drive Marty into work with her every day before school. That old car took them everywhere. Richard even went as far as buying her a new car and my god, did she hate that silly little thing. She said it was too smooth for her. She loved that old truck. 'Can't beat an old steed.' She had always said. I picked it up with her from a junk man's yard. I still don't know why she went with that old thing when she had the money for a better model." Marion explained, her gaze never leaving Eric.

"It does have a lot of good memories, that old car." I smiled at the thought of my mother driving along with me secured in the passenger seat. Holding a warm hot chocolate in my tiny hands after school in the pouring rain. Mum would sing her heart out just to make me smile.

A pang of sadness hit my heart. I looked down at my feet to avoid Marion's sad gaze.

"That's actually really sweet." Eric smiled at me.

"She's a sweet girl, our Marty." John beamed proudly. I offered a smiled back at him and shook my head.

I turned back to my pot of pasta on the stove and dished out the four bowls of dinner, hoping to change the mood. The tension hanging in the air stifling everyone to silence as the sun begun its slow descent from the earth.

As we ate dinner, John explained in vivid detail about his shed and the wood carvings he does. Eric listened attentively whilst Marion and I chatted about her class at school. The bottle of wine between us almost empty. Marion seemed thrilled with herself for having the night off. She deserved a rest. She was your typical housewife. She always done all the cooking and the cleaning. John was never allowed to help her. It wasn't that he didn't try. It was more that fact that he was never allowed.

My mind was buzzing for the moment when they left, and Eric would finally confide in me about whatever it was he wanted to discuss. I was frantic with nerves. It was a struggle to even get through dinner.

"I think we should go home, my love." John cupped Marion's shoulder with his large worn hand.

"Yes, I do have all of those papers to grade, I suppose." She looked down at her solid gold watch against her petite wrist. Her face flushed from the wine she had indulged in. I chuckled at her first instinct to grade the papers rather than relax on her night off.

John took me out to the hall and gave me a hug goodbye whilst Marion stayed in the kitchen and had a private word to Eric. The panic in me rising higher again. What did she say to him?

They walked out and Marion was smiling.

"I will call over sometime tomorrow for a cup of tea so we can eat that cake." She pinched my cheek.

"No worries, Maz." I grunted whilst ripping my face away from her grasp.

She giggled to herself as she hurried to the car behind John.

I was alone again with Eric.

The storm rolled in loudly over us.

## Chapter Eleven

"What did she talk to you about?" I asked, narrowing my eyebrows. I shut the front door behind me. The warmth of the house flooding my skin against the harsh cold from outside.
"She just asked me to take care of you." He shrugged as if it was nothing.
"Right." I drawled. My nails dug deeply into the soft flesh of my palms.
"Can we have that talk now?" he asked as he sat on the sofa.
"Sure." I gritted my teeth and swallowed my fear. I sat down and faced him. My ears ringing, the blood leaving my face. My heart racing with the knots twisting in my stomach. My dinner threatening to come up. Fear oozing from my skin. So, this was the end.
"Marty." he breathed heavily. I raised a hand and put it softly on his leg. He looked at my hand then back up at me. His black hair glistening in the soft light from above.
"I know that I haven't known you for that long, but it feels like I've already known you for years." He traced my blanched knuckles with his finger.
"I feel the same." I said softly. Anxiety rose in my throat. The sick feeling rising with the waves of nerves that continued to pump through my body.
"I think I'm falling for you, Marty." he looked me in the

eyes. I couldn't hide my shock. My eyes went as wide as saucers.

"I feel the exact same way." I confessed without thinking. His breath caught harshly in his throat.

"Are you... sure?" he stuttered. His stare burning into mine.

"Of course." I said softly, trying my hardest to smile.

"Would you like this thing between us to be official? Like a couple type of thing?" he spat out quickly. I felt as if I was going to fall off the couch. My mind racing with the thought.

"Of course, Eric." I repeated. I blushed furiously. My first boyfriend! The panic in me leaving just as quick as the words had left my mouth. My skin cooling with the sudden relief.

"Oh, thank god." He exhaled. His entire body relaxing. He moved closer toward me. His lips met mine hard with a fierce passion, knocking me backward on the couch. My lips danced with his in perfect rhythm. It felt amazing. I had never felt like this before. He was all I wanted. His sweet smell and warm body. He was intoxicating.

A loud clap of thunder broke us apart as the storm rolled in overhead.

"It's going to storm soon." I noted.

"I should probably head home." He sat up and fixed his shirt.

"It's not safe to go out in that." Rain had started pouring down, hammering on the roof loudly.

"I'll be safe." He cupped my face in his hot hands. A bright flash of lightening hit the ground and illuminated sky through the window. My face filled with a worried expression.

"You can stay here!" I suggested eagerly. I didn't want him to go out in the storm. The thunder clapped heavily. I couldn't lose him as well. Memories of the night I had lost mum entering my mind. I shook them away with a quick swivel of my head.

"Are you sure? I have no clothes or anything." He sat up

straight and rubbed a hand over the back of his thin neck. "So?"
"What does that mean?" he said seductively. I felt myself tense up with nerves. My eyebrows raised with panic.
"I – I didn't mean it like that." I stuttered. He laughed deeply.
"I know. It's getting late and we've had a long day ahead tomorrow. Should we head up to bed?" he asked. I nodded. I took his hand and lead him up the stairs and into my bedroom on the left. It was dark from the lack of moonlight. I flicked on the lamp and fairy lights and headed toward my wardrobe to get my pyjamas out.
"I'm just going to get changed." I gestured to the spare bedroom across the hall. He nodded and I went down the hall into the spare bedroom. I brushed my teeth in my bathroom and slipped on my blue pyjamas. I felt like I could be comfortable enough in myself with Eric enough to wear my flannel pyjamas, knowing he wouldn't judge them.
I walked back into the room. Eric was sitting on the edge of the white bed in nothing but his black underwear. His pale slim frame standing out against my white bedding. I almost gasped at the sight. He looked beautiful. My heart soared, breath hitching in my throat. He opened his arms wide for me. I entered them happily. He held me tight as we lay in bed. I took my usual spot under the window and listened to the storm pelt down heavily outside. Eric patted my hair, and I began to finally at peace with myself. The sounds of rain relaxing my tired body. My eyes fluttered close, the sweet allure of sleep drawing me in.
I woke in the morning expecting to find Eric sleeping peacefully next to me, but I didn't. I headed downstairs to see if he was there.
He was nowhere to be found and his car was gone. I looked at the clock. It was only nine and it was still raining heavily outside. I started to mull over the night, worrying that I had dreamt the whole thing. My body shook as the anxiety took over me. I went back upstairs and checked

my phone.
*"Sorry for leaving so early. I had to meet a client for a review. I'll talk soon x."*
The message read.
I breathed a heavy sigh of relief. I didn't dream the whole thing. A laugh left my body as I relaxed. I stared at the ceiling happily. The house was silent in the storm. The rain patted softly and filled the home with its damp scent. Peaceful.
The back door creaked softly.
I headed downstairs toward the noise cautiously.
"Hello?" I called. There was no response. I crept forward, avoiding the creaky floorboards as I made my way to the kitchen only to find a man at the dining table unpacking his black duffle bag.
"Dad!" I yelled excitedly. He turned quickly in defence, this body relaxing when he noticed it was me. his harsh stare calming to his usual loving one.
"There's my baby girl!" he opened his arms and I leapt into them.
His chest was warm as I nuzzled in it. All I wanted to do was tell him about Eric, but I knew he would go crazy if I mentioned anything about a boy. Or anyone being in the house for that matter. I needed to time the moment perfectly. I knew how dad would react to the news.
"Where did you go?" I asked.
"Never you mind about that." He placed his chin on my head and slid his hands up and down my back comfortingly.
"I missed you." I mumbled into his bust before pulling myself away.
"Oh, I missed you too. Something crazy, kid." He held my shoulders. I looked into his deep blue eyes. They crinkled at the sides with happiness.
I looked at the clock again. It hit nine fifteen. I had to be at work by nine forty-five. I tore away from dad and got ready for work.

"I'm so sorry dad. I have to get to work!" I called as I hurried back upstairs.

I didn't see Eric at work, and it was eerily quiet for the morning. Even Greg didn't come in. It was a waste of time being there if I was honest. All the time spent kneeling by the counter, watching as the cars rolled down the street over the wet roads from the downpour that threatened to release again. I locked up the café by myself and headed home.

The moment I got home I began to feel sick to my stomach, almost as if a premonition of bad things to come had warned me to turn around. The rain had eased up, but the dark clouds overhead has threatened to pour down at any second. The smell of damp earth drifted through the cold air.

Bracing myself against the uncomfortable feeling, I headed in the door and hung up my bag. I couldn't see where dad was. I took a cautious step down the hall. The floorboard creaking from under me. Dad's hidden door under the stairs burst open. Within a split second, Dad had pinned me against the wall in one fluid motion. I froze in fear. My body stinging from the hard movement. My back pressed hard against the wall. A family portrait shattered to the ground at our feet.

"Who is he, Marty?" he growled.

"Dad, get off me!" I shouted. I raised my palms to try and push him off.

"Who is he! Who was that boy?" he pressed me harder against the old wall, the plaster creaking with the motion. Photos rattled with the movement.

"Who do you mean? What are you talking about?" I asked, struggling against his grip. My fingers gripping his for dear life.

"That boy, Marty! I have seen everything. Don't you dare even consider lying to me." He pressed my body to the wall harder. The tips of his ears red with anger. I scrunched my eyes to avoid his gaze

"He is a friend, dad!" I lied.

"He is not a friend Martha. I've seen it all." He pushed me harder again. The wall creaked again as if it were about to give way at any moment. My skin burnt under his grasp on my arms. Blood draining from them.

"Dad, please. You're hurting me." I almost squealed with pain. A tingling sensation began to form in the palms of my hands. Tears flooded my eyes. The familiar sting only adding to the pain in my body.

"I lost your mother, Marty, and I sure as hell aren't losing you!" he let me go cautiously.

"You aren't going to lose me, Dad. Jesus, calm down." I rubbed my arms where he had pinned me.

"I saw everything, Martha." he spat at me. I narrowed my eyes at him. The tears held at bay now spilling over my cheeks.

"How? Dad! How did you see it all?" I gritted my teeth. My pent-up anger rising.

He grabbed my arm and wrenched me into the lounge. My feet dragged behind us as hauled me behind him. His strong hand grabbed my face and moved it to the direction of the corner of the room at the tv cabinet.

"You don't think I wouldn't watch out for you whilst I was away, Marty." he threw me forward, I stumbled but regained my balance. A small little camera sat poking out from next the tv, barely visible to anyone unless you were to search for it.

"You're insane! You are actually mental! How long has that been there?" I shouted, turning to look at him. How could he watch me?

"You are disgusting Marty" dad growled again "You are nothing but a whore! A common street whore!" he threw his hands behind him.

"I am not!" I shouted back in defence of myself.

"Dirty little slut! Just like your mother." he lunged at me. It was like something in him had snapped and every bit of rage he held broke out of him with every word he expressed. I felt my eyes stinging with angry tears. He had never spoken to me like this. How dare he treat me like

this! After all of the years I had kept his secret and\
disregarded anything bad anyone had said about him. They were right. They all were.

"Dad, please." I begged him to listen to me. He raised his hand and slapped me harshly across the cheek. Tears began streaming down against my hot stinging skin.

Dad stepped back from me. Breathing heavily as he stared wildly at me as if I were pray caught in his web.

"No more, Marty. I don't want that boy here ever again. You hear me?" he breathed out heavily as he waved a finger at me before leaving to go back under the stairs.

I couldn't breathe. My mind was racing, and my heart was broken. I never thought he would do that to me. Let alone could do that to me. my heart thundered; tears clouded my vision. I couldn't breathe. I needed to escape this prison.

I grabbed my handbag off the hook and ran outside. I couldn't be in the house any longer.

I didn't know where to run to. I got in my truck and drove away. Leaving dad far behind me.

*Chapter Twelve*

I cried my eyes out the entire ride into town. Sobbing into my jacket sleeve, tears had drenched the dark material. The rain began falling heavily as I drove through the empty streets. I stopped my car out the front of Eric's green town house before trying to clean myself up. I wiped my eyes on my sleeve, the tears staining my blue shirt underneath dark. I collected myself and headed inside. I knocked on the red door. I could see him coming toward the door through the frosted glass panels.
I broke down the moment he had opened the door. Feeling more broken than I had ever felt before. My heart shattered into a million jiggered pieces. Tears began to stream down my tired face. Why was I even here? He shouldn't see me like this.
"Marty!" he exclaimed at the sight of me. He wrapped his warm arms around me and brought me inside. I sobbed into the soft dark fabric of his shirt.
"I was just coming to see you." He said softly as he patted my hair whilst he held me tightly against him.
"Dad came back, and he was going insane, and he didn't like that I was with you and then he hit me, and I don't know what to do, Eric. I can't go back home." I blurted out, sobbing into my hands.
"What?" he asked confusedly. His hand grazing the tender flesh that dad had struck. The warm touch bringing another sharp sting of pain. My shoulders ached from

being pressed against the wall.

"Dad. He comes and goes all the time, and he came back today. He must have seen that I was with you, and he went berserk and hit me, and I just ran away! I had nowhere else to go. I'm sorry." I sobbed harder at the fact that I was breaking down in front of Eric then the fact that I was heartbroken. I looked pathetic but it was too late to leave.

"Come sit down." He gestured toward the couch in the living room. It was small, black and hard. I sat down and tried to compose myself.

Eric left the room for a while, and I gasped for air. My head lowered between my legs. What had I done? I had told him Dad was still here! He was going to think I was the one who was insane. This was all a mistake. I should have just listened to dad. I should never have trusted anyone. I needed to run.

I could hear him talking softly as I bounced my leg up and down on the couch with nerves. It was now or never.

He came back in the grey room with a glass of water, and I began to cry again at the thought of my mistake. I cried at the fact that this poor boy had chosen me to love and here I was having a breakdown in his living room about something that he had no idea was even happening. I sounded mental. I was mental.

I continued to let every ounce of my heart out to Eric through my tears and he held me as a cried. Rocking me back and forth to sooth me.

"It's alright, Marty." he cooed "I still love you."

Hi sweet affirmation only made me feel worse. How could he love something so broken?

A car door slammed outside, and I could hear hurried footfalls come toward the house.

I wiped my eyes on the back of my sleeve. Beginning to feel the bittersweet allure of numbness as I pulled away from Eric.

Eric got up and opened the door for the guests. I stared off into the wall. Focusing on nothing but my thoughts of not being good enough for him. My eyes burning from my

endless tears that had now dried up. A feeling of numbness overtook me. I couldn't move. My mind was empty.
Marion materialised in front of me.
"Marty?" she said my name softly. I didn't respond. I stared straight through her at the cream wall. "Marty, can you hear us?" John pinched my shoulder.
I couldn't respond, my mouth wired shut.
"Marty, your safe now. Come back to us, honey." Marion whispered. Her hands ran through my hair, just as she did when I would have breakdown when I was a child. She pulled me closer to her chest and rested my head on her shoulder.
"I have you. You're safe now." She whispered into my ear. My body was frozen, and my mind was weak. I couldn't do anything but watch her. Her heart breaking through her voice.
"John, she's gone again." her voice croaked. I could hear the sadness in her tone, but I couldn't respond. She pulled away and searched my face for any hint of feeling.
Uncle John reached down from in front of me and scooped me up in his arms. I didn't move or say anything as he carried me into the back of Marion's small work car. Marion spoke to Eric and assured him I would be okay. I couldn't make out exactly what else she was saying to him. I didn't care to listen.
Marion opened the door to her small car and sat next to me in the back seat. Her gentle hand patting my hair softly as I looked blankly out of the opposite window to avoid Eric's gaze. Her thin arms reached over me to put on my seatbelt.
"Everything is going to be okay, Marty. We are going to get you the help you need this time, okay?" she tried to soothe me as she put my head down on her shoulder.
We drove for hours in silence. I had no idea where we were going but I didn't care. The further away from home, the better.

The freeway was quiet and dry as we drove to our destination. Clouds rolled overhead as we travelled beneath them. The dark mass matching the feelings raging inside me.

We pulled up in front of a large dull grey building. The numbness began to wear off as I straightened myself from Marion. John left us in the car whilst he went into the building.

He came back with two men in white scrubs. Panic coursed through me.

me and my flight sense took over. This couldn't be real. "No!" I shouted "No! No! No!" I fought to get out of the car and flee, but Marion held me back by the shoulders. Her manicured nails digging into my flesh as I struggled.

"Marty, please." She begged for me to be still and not resist.

The nurses opened the door of the car.

"Hello, Martha." The blonde one said kindly. "My name is Seth. Would you like to come inside?"

"No. Don't you dare touch me." I threatened, kicking out at the door.

"Marty, please." Marion pleaded sadly, her grip tightening on my shoulders.

"No! I'm not insane!" I shouted.

"We are here only to help you, Martha." Seth said soothingly. I shook my head wildly.

"Your father has been dead a long time, Marty." John said extending a limp hand out for me to take.

"No, he hasn't. He's at my house! You're lying to me! He hit me!" I shook my head. They were lying to coax me inside. I just knew it.

"Martha, please come inside." the other man spoke. He was shorter than Seth with deep dark skin.

"No." I gritted my teeth and shook my head. My eyes contacted John's sad brown ones.

He gave me a small smile and tried to help me out of the car. I wasn't getting out the car without a fight.

Seth and the other nurse each took one of my legs and

pulled me from the car. Their grip moved up to my armpits from my legs. They dragged me into the building with one arm each.

I kept screaming no but no one listened. My head was ringing from exhaustion.

"How could you do this!" I screamed. I turned my head to look back at Marion and John.

"I hate you! Fuck you!" I cried. More tears hitting my eyes. My aching body dragging behind the brutes who carried me.

"I'm sorry, Marty, but it was for the best." Marion called from back at the car. She began to sob into Uncle John's shirt as I was pulled further away from them.

"I hate you!" I called again.

How could they do this to me. I wasn't lying! I was telling the truth. Why would no one listen to me?

"Let's take you to your new room, Martha." Seth spoke softly as he led me down a hall. I had begun to calm down and was no longer resisting them. The other nurse had left us to stop by the front desk. The women behind the protected glass avoiding my acidic gaze.

Seth led me through multiple hallways and past new people who stared and gawked at me as I walked by. Seth had one arm looped in mine so I couldn't run, no matter how much I wanted to. I pulled the other one over my stomach. My work sneakers squeaked on the white lino floors as we headed down more halls. Every door was closed but the one to our right.

"Here is your new room, Marty." Seth led me into the clean white room with nothing but a hospital bed in it. The only feature of the room was a blindly bright orange feature wall.

"Thanks." I mumbled. My will to fight fleeting the further I entered the room. There was no point. Maybe I was insane after all.

"Get some rest. We will speak in the morning." Seth shut the door behind him and left me alone. I explored my room. It was small with a white board on the wall and a pin board above my bed. The bed looked uncomfortable and cold. There was a bathroom with a shower and toilet to the right of the room and that was it. A white plastic clock was bolted to the wall.

I walked up to the whiteboard.

"Welcome, Martha!" it read in blue ink.

I scoffed and rubbed it off on my sleeve. This wasn't a welcome I needed nor wanted.

The bathroom was small as I stepped into it. There was no shower curtain. Only a pane of thick glass to stop the water from flooding out. I sighed before undressing. The heat lamp above helping to keep my exhausted body warm. The tap creaked as I turned it on.

The warm water ran over my body. I let the water rinse away all my worries. Focusing on nothing but the heat of the water.

I walked out of the bathroom and into the bedroom. A pair of soft grey pyjamas sat folded neatly on the foot of the plain white bed.

The bed welcomed me as I curled up in it. I held back my tears as I brought the blanket over my head for warmth. I slept a solid sleep until nine am. Not a single dream entered my mind.

## Chapter Thirteen

"Good morning, Martha." Seth opened the door whilst smiling at me. He wheeled in a trolley with a breakfast tray on the top and a large bag underneath. I sat up in my stiff bed, avoiding his gaze.
"Your Aunt has just brought you a bag of clothes and a few belongings. I thought it would make you feel a little more normal during your time here." He smiled at me. His green eyes welcoming.
"Thank you." I said sadly. I would never be 'normal' again.
He left me alone in the room to eat. I ate the bland cereal and drank the orange juice next to it. Its acidic taste coating my throat. I gritted my teeth at the sour taste left in my mouth.
As I unpacked the yellow bag, I searched desperately for my phone. I pulled all the clothes onto the floor and ran my hands roughly through my hair with despair. I needed to talk to Eric.
"They take your phone." A gruff female voice said. My gaze flying up at the doorway. My heart raced with fear.
A short girl with boyish teal hair stood leaning against my orange wall with her arms crossed. A red rose tattoo peeking out of her black sleeve on her wrist.
"Why do they take it?" I asked her.
"So, we can't plot our escape." She rolled her green hazel eyes.
"Right. And you are?" I stood up. My posture

straightening stiffly.

"Name's Kresley Redwood. Yours?" she stretched out her small olive toned hand out for me to shake. She stood a good foot shorter than me although she did look rather strong for her small size.

"Marty Green." I shook her hand back.

"Nice to meet ya. What are you in for?" she bent down to pick up my stuff.

"I ahh…" I trailed off as I bent down to stop her.

"Don't worry. I'm not a freak." She raised her hands in a surrender.

"Thanks?" I said, confused by her movements.

"No worries. Now what are you in for?" she asked again. Her voice hoarse.

"I had a breakdown." I admitted. Why was she so pushy?

"Me too." She sighed. Kresley wrapped her hands around her hips. Watching as I picked up my belongings.

"Are you alright?" I asked her.

"I'll get there one day, I suppose." She shrugged. Her broad shoulders slumping to the right.

I nodded. Kresley helped me put my belongings into a single cupboard and offered to show me around the facility.

She led me down all the spotless white halls and pointed out various rooms that they use.

The halls were white and bleak. The fluorescent lights bouncing off the shiny floor. The smell of cleaning products rife in the musty air. My shoes squeaked against the plastic-coated floors.

Kresley pointed out each room as we passed it with an air of knowledge. It was as if she ruled the place. I knew I wouldn't remember where anything was, but I was very grateful for her company. I was going to need it to survive in here.

We went in a full circle around the entirety of the small centre and then back to my room where a doctor stood waiting at my bed. She was tall with cherry red hair and a warm smile. Her skin wrinkled. She looked older than she probably was.

"Hello, Martha. I see you have met Kresley." She had a high voice.

"Yes." I didn't want to say much to anyone. I only wanted to escape and go back home.

"Good. Shall we go have a little chat?" she gestured to the hall outside. I nodded and she led me down the hall to the left into an office. I stood a fair amount taller than her.

"Take a seat." She waved to a plastic red chair in the corner. The room was green and felt childish with rainbow flowers painted messily on the walls.

"Why am I here?" I asked roughly as I sat in the hard seat.

"You're here because your aunt and uncle were worried about you and your mental state." She sat across from me at a desk.

"I'm fine." I sighed, leaning back in the stiff chair.

"I know, Martha." She smiled at me with her head tilted to the left.

"My name is Marty." I corrected her.

"Okay. Marty it is then." she shuffled some paperwork "whilst you are here, we are going to help you. We are going to help you with all your past trauma and help you cope with day-to-day life. You gave your family quite a fright yesterday."

My mind went to Eric, and I swallowed the hard lump that had rose whilst I looked down to avoid her gaze. I had ruined my first ever relationship. No one would ever love me again.

"Your phone has been going off like crazy though." The woman laughed.

"You have my phone?" I looked up at her eagerly. My eyes darted around the office with angst.

"Yes. Would you like to read the messages?" she raised her thin ginger eyebrows.

"Yes. Please." I spat out anxiously. My heart bet faster against my ribcage.

"If you promise me you will comply with your treatment, I

will let you read them just this once."

"Yes, whatever you want." I was eager to read to see if Eric sent anything to me after everything that had happened in the last twenty-four hours.

"Here." she handed me my silver phone from a drawer in her desk.

I ignored all the other various messages on the phone until I found the one I wanted.

*"I am so sorry about all this, Marty. I really am. I meant it when I said I love you. Everyone needs a little help sometimes. I'll see you soon. X"* It read.

I immediately felt better. My anxiety and doubts left my body for a brief moment. I really didn't deserve this man. The expression on my face blank to conceal my sudden relief.

There was message from an unknown number.

*"I know."* It read. I knew it was dad. I hunched my shoulders with displeasure.

"Take it." I tossed it back to the woman hastily. I had seen all that I had wanted.

"You seem rather tense, Marty. Are you okay?" She cocked her head to the side, observing me.

"I just don't think I need to be here, to be honest with you." I looked her in the eye. Her wrinkled skin coated in heavy makeup around her deep hazel eyes.

"Well, Marty. You are here because you had a breakdown, and you need some help to cope with the trauma you have been through. Which is perfectly normal after all that you have been through over the years."

"I haven't been through any major trauma" I pressed. She blinked her almond eyes slowly.

"You have been through some serious trauma, Martha. After your mother died, you were desperate for anything to do with your father, so you created a narrative. You believed that he would live in secret under the house, and you would get him food and supplies. But Marty, your father died in a house fire in a town no longer than a month after your mother died. You know this deep down. We are going to help you accept it."

"You're lying. No one knew about my supply runs." I was shocked.

"According to your aunt you always used to talk in your sleep about them."

"I could have just been dreaming." I furrowed my brows, turning my head from her to avoid her pitying gaze.

"You could have been." She shrugged her right shoulder.

"Who are you anyway?" I asked, glaring at her.

"Didn't I introduce myself?" she laughed to herself "I'm Linda. I am your councillor for the duration of your time here."

"How long will I be here?"

"As long as you need to be I'm afraid." She offered a small smile.

"Well, that's great doc because look, I'm cured! Good work doctor Linda!" I said sarcastically and headed for the door.

"Martha, we will meet every day for 2 hours in the morning and in the evening. We will get there and get you ready to go home once more." she assured me.

"Thanks, Linda. But I don't need your help!" I reached for the door only to find it was locked. I pulled it again to make sure. It didn't budge.

"Here, I will take you back to your room."

Linda stood and unlocked the door with her plastic id card. The door buzzed as she swiped the card over it. The bolt unlocked with a clink.

Linda held the door open for me and I walked out past her. Her flowery perfume finding its way into my nose. A longing for the field hit my mind.

I followed her back down the hall to my cell.

The halls were empty as we walked silently back to my room. I didn't want to talk to her. I didn't want to talk to anyone here.

"Try and make the best of your time here, Marty. Please know that we only want to help you." Linda said as we got to my room.

"I'll try." I said dryly. I opened the door and slammed it behind me.

I didn't feel bad for my behaviour toward Linda. She treated me like a child. Everyone always did.

"I am not a child." I mumbled angrily to myself as I turned away from the door.

A white plastic lunch tray with four little sandwiches was left on my bed for lunch. They were all rather dry, but I ate them anyway. I missed Frank's fresh café sandwiches. A pang of sadness hit my chest.

It was going to be a long time before I could even think of going home. I just knew it. The longing to go home overtook me as I lay down on the hard bed. The eery silence of my room only amplified the thoughts in my head. I was alone. Nobody would know I was here. Nobody would care that I was here.

I felt more alone than I had ever felt before.

I adjusted my pillows underneath my head. The fabric crinkling loudly as I shifted them. My eyes stared at the wall, but my mind was elsewhere. I was a million miles away in my own thoughts. The blissful sensation of being numb overcame me again and I welcomed it once more. Falling into its sweet embrace.

## Chapter Fourteen

Dinner that night was just as plain as the lunch they served. Meat with a selection of three veg.
Kresley had come to visit me before dinner and divulged stories of her past experiences in centres, arousing me from my numbness. She had been to three different centres in her time, but she said this was the nicest by far as it wasn't nearly as strict as ones she had been admitted to in the past. Kresley suffered from extreme anger attacks and had trouble controlling them. I felt bad for her. She seemed like such a nice girl.
I sat alone on my cold hard bed when the night nurse came in to check on me. It was the other doctor that helped drag me in to the centre. I instantly resented him for locking me in here.
"Hello." He smiled warmly at me.
"Hello." I mumbled back, not in the mood to talk to anyone. I glared at the orange wall.
"I am Adam. I'm here to take your ob.'s and make sure everything is going smoothly for you." He put a hand to his chest.
"Okay." I sneered.
"I have your schedule for your time here. You are to follow this exactly as it reads." He passed me a laminated piece of paper.
I looked over the fresh schedule, still warm from the laminator.

*"9 am: Wake up and shower time.*
*9:30am -10am: Breakfast*
*10am- 11 am: Outside time with Linda.*
*11am-12pm: Meditation with Linda.*
*12pm- 1pm: Lunch.*
*1pm- 2pm: Arts and Craft.*
*2pm-4pm: Quiet time.*
*4pm- 6pm: Therapy with Linda.*
*6pm- 7pm: Dinner.*
*7pm- 9pm: Personal time.*
*9pm: Bedtime."*

"Does everyone get a lot of time with Linda?" I asked after noticing how I was to spend so much time with her.
"Linda deals with childhood trauma and because you have repressed a lot of yours, she had requested to offer you the most support she can." Adam wheeled a blue blood pressure machine to my right side as I sat on the stiff bed.
"How long will I be here then?" I asked.
He looked at me with his big brown eyes. "Until you're better."
"What if I'm better tomorrow." I suggested.
"No" he chuckled. "it'll be about a month at the very least."
"Great. A whole month of being a prisoner." I sighed and rolled my eyes. I really didn't want to hear that.
"It's for the best, Martha. You will get the help you need to flourish in the outside world." Adam reassured me. He wrapped the blue band of the blood pressure machine around my arm. The blood pressure machine squeezed tightly around my bicep. My mind went to Marion and John.
"How long have my family had me on the register here?" I asked Adam. He moved toward the steel trolley he had wheeled in covered in medical supplies.
"For around five or so years." He admitted. Looking into my mouth with a popsicle stick.
"Really? Since I turned eighteen?" I felt enraged. Why

couldn't they talk to me about this? They didn't even believe me to check that dad wasn't real.
"Yes, Martha" he held out a small plastic cup to me. "These are to be taken."
I looked inside the little cup. "What are they?"
"They are just a standard Anti- Depressant. Linda has prescribed them for you to help take the edge off your pain."
I peered down at the tiny pill in the cup. I considered not taking it but if it helped me get out of here faster, I would do anything.
I slipped the white tablet into my mouth and swallowed it dry.
Adam made me lift my tongue to assure it was swallowed. He smiled when he saw it wasn't hidden in my mouth.
Adam continued his check on me and left me alone to rest. My mind was reeling with hurt and anger.
How could they do this to me? They were supposed to look after me. Not dump me here when things got tough. I felt the hot sting of tears hit my eyes.
"They're lying." I said to myself repeatedly, pressing my head in my pillow and crying myself softly to sleep.

I woke up to a loud knock on my door alerting me it was time to get up.
The light swam in from the small window of my room. I missed my bedroom window. Rain drizzled softly and patted against the thick glass. I couldn't take my eyes of it whilst I scraped my long hair into a messy ponytail.
I dressed in a pair of black jeans and a fluffy lilac jumper that Marion had packed and went to the dining hall where I ate some plain cereal and tropical fruit.
Linda met me in the hall wearing a red winter coat over her white scrubs. It was colder in the wards than my room. The fluff of my fuzzy jumper helped to keep me warm. The soft cotton felt smooth against my skin, bringing comfort in a time of need.
"Good morning, Marty." she greeted me cheerfully.

"Good morning, Linda." I said stiffly.
"How did you sleep?" she asked kindly.
"Well. Thanks." Her gaze wondered over me. I shifted uncomfortably from foot to foot.
"Shall we go outside today?" Linda led me out to a small outside area. There was nothing but a park picnic table and freshly mowed green grass. A fence stood high around the centre to stop anyone escaping. It felt more like a prison than a place to help anyone. The rain had stopped its drizzle, and the sun had begun to beam in the sky. The light wooden bench seemed dry enough to sit on. The worn wood creaked as I placed my weight on it.
"Your aunt said you enjoyed being outside, so I added it to your schedule." She smiled at me as she sat on the grey worn wood of the table.
"Thanks." I mumbled.
I sat down slowly across from her. Linda looked at me cheerfully.
"I am only here to help you, Marty."
"I'm not here for your help" I snapped "I'm here because I was forced here, Linda."
"I understand you are quite upset Marty, but I believe you have a lot of repressed trauma and memories we need to sort out before you can return home to normalcy."
I looked away from her as I began scowling.
"The sooner we open up, the sooner you can return home to your new boyfriend." She said jokingly.
"What?" how did she know about Eric?
"Your uncle mentioned you met a boy recently. Would you like to tell me about him?" she asked.
I considered not telling her anything, but her words rang in my head. Maybe I could speed up being here by opening myself up to her. I felt the words gather in my throat. My airways growing tight as I tried to force out the words.
I told her everything. How I met him and how it made me feel so much better on the inside. It all spilled out of me without me realising.
"Well Linda, his name is Eric. He had just moved down

from the city. He is an accountant. I met him through my job at the local cafe. It was like an instant attraction towards him. I couldn't stop thinking of him. It was nice to focus on someone else for once."
She smiled and nodded whilst I spoke about him.
"Well, he seems like a lovely guy." She gushed with her hazel eyes blazing.
I felt a bit lighter after talking. Maybe I could tell her everything after all.
*"You can't say anything about your dad. He will literally kill you."* I thought to myself.
"What about your other friends? Do you have many others?" Linda asked.
"No. I have no friends." I admitted glumly.
"Have you tried to make friends with any local people around your age?" she asked.
"They don't like me." I looked down at my hands in my lap to avoid her gaze. Sadness filling my body. My mind wandered to the girl from the restaurant. She would be glad not to be friends with me right now.
"And why is that?"
"They all speak about me as if I am some broken lonely monster. That I'm just a mess from a messed-up family." I wrapped my arms around myself for comfort.
"I am sure they don't believe that, Marty." she tried to reassure me. She moved her body toward me over the table.
"They do. I've heard them. So, I stick to myself." I shrugged my left shoulder.
"Fair enough. I see you have been taken in by Kresley." She tilted her head to the left and changed the subject.
"Yeah." I nodded.
"She's a lovely girl. Very much like you. You would be good friends with her."
"Noted." I spoke. That was reassuring at least.
"Now, tell me more about yourself." Linda relaxed her body and waited for my answer.
"What do you want to know?"

"Everything about you." She smiled.
"What do you mean?" I asked.
"Tell me your name, hobbies or favourite things. I don't mind. Just tell me about you. I want to get to know you. We can be friends if you like." She grinned, folding her hands over each other on the wooden table in front of her.
"My name is Martha May Green. I am twenty-three and I love being outside and surrounded by nature."
"Good, tell me more." She raised her eyebrows attentively.
"I work at a local café and formerly a supermarket. I don't have many friends, but I do have a close friend. He's name is Eric, and he is my boyfriend. Well, he was." I put my head down sadly with self-doubt.
"Did he break up with you, Marty?" Linda asked calmly.
"No, not really. He called my aunt who brought me here after I had the break down over the incident with my father. He wouldn't want to be with someone like me now. I'm too broken. Too hard for him to love." I admitted. Linda looked at me pitifully.
"You aren't broken, Marty. You just need some help. Everyone needs help sometimes" Linda reached over and held my shoulder reassuringly.
"Thank you, Linda." I was grateful for her comfort. The feeling of my heartbeat thundering picked up against my chest.
"Should we go over by the grass and meditate for an hour? I thought it would be good for you seeing as you enjoy nature that we spend time in it for you."
"I would like that very much. Thank you, Linda." I was shocked by her kindness. Maybe I could fully open up to her about dad's secret if she would believe me.
We moved over to a patch of cement by the grass that had dried in the suns growing warmth and Linda guided me through a mediation. She directed my breathing. Her calming voice instructing my mind as I let go of my worries. The smell of warm grass bringing with it the sensation of laying in the field by my house. A lump

caught in my throat at the thought of my field. The thought of running through the soft autumn blooms brought a smile to my face.

I felt so calm afterwards. It felt fantastic. The calming sound of her voice washed comforting waves over me. The sun warmed my skin as a large smile creeped across my cool face. I smiled for the first time since my arrival here.

"Better?" Linda asked.

"Much better." I nodded happily.

After the meditation, Linda walked me to the dining hall for lunch. It was colder in the large white hall filled with metal tables than it was outside. I shuddered from the cool change.

I sat at the end of one table away from everyone. A small plump nurse handed me a plate with a sandwich on it and a glass of cold water.

"Thank you." I said lightly. She smiled back at me and moved to the next person. Her tight blonde curls swaying with the movement

I investigated my sandwich. Ham and salad. I sighed and took my first bite. The overpowering taste of mayonnaise stung my mouth. My face contorted with the unsavoury taste.

"How's it going?" Kresley's rough voice startled me. I watched her as she sat herself down next to me.

"Fine. Yourself?" I asked through my mouthful of sandwich. I was starving after mediation.

"That's good! I'm alright. Just had therapy." She pointed her thumb over her broad shoulder to the double entry way doors. Her short blue hair getting caught around it.

"Nice." I didn't know what else to say. We ate our sandwiches in silence together but were content with each other's company.

The nurse came and cleared out plates from us. She told us it was time for our next schedule item. Her voice sounded sweet as sugar.

"What have you got next?" Kresley asked me.

"Arts and Crafts." I remembered.

"Me too! I'll walk with you to the craft room!" she said cheerfully. She rose too quickly from the table. Her chair tumbled to the floor. Other patients looked around, startled by the loud sound.

"Oh, shut up, Billy." She yelled to one boy who snickered at her fallen chair. His face blanched white as he turned in on himself with fear.

We walked down the corridors to another white room. There were six tables, and each already had someone at them. Kresley sat next to a young boy who moved as soon as she sat down across from him. He scowled at her loudly before hurrying off.

"Rude." She muttered to herself and patted the seat next to her.

"Welcome." The nurse said. I looked up to see Adam looking at me from the other side of the table.

"Hello, Adam." I greeted him.

"It's good to see you smiling today, Marty." he noted happily.

"Better than feeling sorry for myself." I shrugged.

"What would you like to do?" he asked. His smile genuine.

"What can I do?" I furrowed my brows. How was I meant to know what to do?

"Well, Marty. In here you can paint or colour or draw. Whichever you prefer."

"I'll paint I guess." I nodded. Adam placed a pad of pure white paper down in front of me with a pack of soft water colour paints.

"What will you paint for us?" he asked me cheerfully. His almond eyes reflecting his smile.

"I don't know yet." I said softly. I had never really painted before. I used to ice flowers on the cakes in the café and they always turned out okay. Maybe I could paint some flowers.

I dripped my wet brush into the light purple paint block and began to paint a small sprig of lavender. I dotted the purple paint in a line and continued to expand them. The purple dots bleeding into each other and creating different shades of colour. I cleared my brush on a piece of paper towel and moved it into the green paint. I painted a small green stem at the bottom of the purple flowers. I was pleased with my outcome.

I glanced over at Kresley who had a canvas in front of her. She was painting a portrait of a woman in black and white. I couldn't make out who it was yet, but it was beautiful. She really was talented. Her brush strokes precise as she swiped her brush over the canvas.

I looked back at my own lonely sprig of lavender on the white page. I continued my painting of wildflowers until Adam announced that it was now quiet time. Kresley went her room for the bathroom, and I went to my own.

I walked into the lonely bedroom and noticed a small package on the bed.

## Chapter Fifteen

It was wrapped in brown paper. I opened it carefully. A book was wrapped perfectly in the middle. I lifted it up. It was the fantasy book I was reading at home. There was a yellow post it notes stuck on the front cover.
*"Your aunt gave us this to give to you. She said it was your favourite. – Linda."*
I smiled down at my book and opened the page to where my homemade bookmark was.
I had just begun reading when my door opened and startled me.
"Hey!" Kresley waltzed into my room.
"What are you doing here?" I asked her. Not taking my eyes off my book.
"It's quiet time. I thought I would come hang out with you." She pointed both her hands at me.
"Are you allowed to do that?" I looked up at her and furrowed my brows.
"As long as the door is open, they shouldn't have a problem with it. I wouldn't care if they did anyway." She shrugged it off.
She sat down on my bed and relaxed her body.
"Right." I didn't fully believe her, but I was grateful for the company none the less. We sat together on the bed and told stories of our past. Kresley was freshly twenty from a town over three hours away. She had been here twice as she was deemed a danger to herself and others after she lost control during a fight with her boyfriend. She said it

was a toxic relationship for the both of them, but she felt it was her fault she was back in here. Kresley talked for the entirety of the two hours allocated quiet time which I didn't mind. It was nice to hear someone else's stories. She told tales of old partners and old people she knew. She spoke so highly of every single one of them. No one was ever a villain in her stories.
"I am very glad to see you two are getting along." Linda stood in the doorway, breaking the ambiance of calm Kresley had created.
"Hi, Linda!" Kresley gushed up at her.
"Hello, Kresley." she smiled at her but moved her gaze to me "Marty, It's time for your therapy."
I joined Linda at the door, and we walked to her office. I feared therapy. I didn't think I would ever need it. I felt like I was coping just fine on my own.
I sat in the hard, plastic red chair and focused on Linda. She sat across from me with her fresh notebook and pen at the ready.
"Now, Marty. I want you to tell me everything about your father." She peered down at me.
I began to panic. No one knew his secret but me.
"You can trust me. I am here to help you with this." Linda spoke warmly. I had begun to feel a bond forming. I felt safe in her presence. Much like I did with Eric.
"I can't." I confessed shakily. My legs began bouncing up and down. My fingernails digging into the soft pads of my palms.
"No one will know anything. It's only you and I in here."
I took a breath and swallowed hard.
"My father..." I paused and looked at Linda. She smiled at me and nodded for me to continue.
"My father, Richard Green. He lives in my house with me but always goes into hiding when someone comes over.
He is ashamed of my mother's death. Yet he believes it is all her fault. When she died, he went into hiding. No one knew where he was, but I always did. He would visit me at Marion's house late at night and give me a list of supplies

and some money. I would go to the supermarket and get them for him. I used to tell John I was going out for a bike ride. I would ride the supplies over to the house and deliver them to dad. He used to hunt for meat and grow his own vegetables by the forest near our house, but he never went into the town during the day. He only came in at night to wake me up for the lists so that no one would see him. When I turned eighteen John and Marion allowed me to move into the house by myself. But they didn't know I wasn't by myself. Dad was always there with me. He cooked and cleaned during the day whilst also working from home and I would go to work in town and come home. He is my best friend in the entire world, my dad."

"So, your father. Is he at the house now?" Linda queried.

"Yes. Sometimes he disappears for a few months or weeks but then he always comes back."

"Right." She said as she scribbled down notes. "How often does he usually go away for?"

"Sometimes a week, sometimes a month." I shrugged my left shoulder. A bubble of panic began to grow in the pit of my stomach. She didn't believe me. I really did sound mental.

"And does anyone else know he is in the house with you?"

"No. He told me that if I ever told anyone he would hurt me and that they would take him away from me for good." I confessed, looking down at my knees. I shook with nerves. Silently praying dad didn't plant a bug in my phone, wherever it was now.

Linda scribbled on her notepad again. The scratching sound echoing in the still silence.

"Linda, he is alive. I'm not lying." I looked into her eyes as I told her. Pleading with her to believe me. To believe I wasn't crazy. I knew I wasn't.

"Marty, what you are experiencing is a form of post-traumatic stress disorder. You created the narrative of your father still being alive so you could cope with the fact that he abandoned you."

"No, I didn't. He really is alive. You can go search the

house. He will still be there. He even sent me a text!" I laughed and shook my head with disbelief. Why could no one believe me?

"Would you like to see an article from the paper the night your father died?" she offered.

"Sure." I didn't believe her any more than she believed me.

Linda stood and walked to her desk. She came back with a cutting of an old newspaper. The title stood out clearly in black ink against the yellowing paper.

*"Local man dies in house fire."* It read.

*"Local man Richard Green has died tragically just less than a month after the death of his late wife Maree. The cause of the fire is yet to be known, but the local police department believe it may have been deliberate. Richard leaves behind an eleven-year-old daughter who will be raised by her aunt and uncle in light of these horrific events."*

I reread the article five times. It was impossible. Dad was still alive. He was always with me. He couldn't have died. A lump rose in my throat as my heart fell into my stomach.

"Have you finished with it?" Linda asked softly.

"Yes." I tossed it back to her as if it had burnt me.

"And what do you think?" she pressed.

"He didn't die Linda! He is still in the house! He lives in the basement! The door is under the stairs!" I shouted angrily.

"Martha, calm down. I know this is hard to hear but I am telling the truth. You read the article. I also have a copy of the death certificate if you would like to see that as well." Linda stood over me.

"So am I! He is still there." I waved my hand out in front of me. I felt the hot sting of angry tears hit the back of my eyes. I let them fall onto my face. Linda sat back down and put her hands on my shoulders. My face burned with anger and hurt. My hands balled into fists, and I stabbed my nails into my palms, desperate to feel a different form of pain.

"I am not lying, Linda. Please believe me!" I begged.

I wished for this all to be some sick twisted joke but deep down, I knew it wasn't.

"I'm going to teach you how to cope with your grief, Marty. You can trust me." She cooed. Linda rubbed her soft hands down my cheek to clear away the tears that had fallen onto them.

I sobbed softly into my hands. I wasn't insane. Why did everyone believe I was?

## Chapter Sixteen

"What are you painting?" I leant over to look at Kresley's canvas. It had been a week since I confessed everything to Linda. We spent our days talking through everything and she taught me coping mechanisms to help with my pain. I was taught to count to ten every time I started to get overwhelmed and if that didn't work, I was to focus on the world around me and take note of six different things I could feel, smell, see or hear. This came in handy when it came to the dining hall. Some people liked to be very loud, and it was often the ones who needed the attention that was cause an uproar. I knew it wasn't their fault. It was just their way of getting the help they wanted quickly.
I still wasn't fully convinced that my dad was dead.
"None of your business." Kresley poked her short tongue out and dotted a blub of grey paint on my nose.
I contorted my face as I wiped it on her shoulder. The light red shirt she was wearing now marked with a muddy grey mess.
"Gross!" she shouted.
Adam turned to us but looked away when he seen her smiling at me. a slight smile crossed his face.
"You really are gross, Green." Kresley had taken to calling me by my last name. I didn't mind. I was sick of being called Marty. I actually missed being called kid. I felt anger bubble as I thought of my so-called family. I breathed the anger away like Linda had taught me.

"Says you!" I looked down at my wildflower painting. The soft blue of the flower reminding me of my mother. I smiled to myself at the thought of her.

I thought about my mother the entirety of my quiet time. Kresley continued telling me a story of her and an ex, but I couldn't concentrate on anything but my mum.

My mind wandered to the night of her death.

Did she know it was her time?

The night she had died, she gave me a long kiss on the forehead as if she knew it was the last kiss she would ever have. It was as if she was pushing all of the love, she had into me.

A pang of guilt hit my chest. What would she think of me being here now? I knew she wouldn't have put me in here, she would have believed me.

Before I knew it, Linda was at my door.

"Are you ready, Martha?" she smiled as Kresley waltzed passed her.

"Yes, Linda." I rose and followed her down the freezing halls.

We sat in her bright office, and I looked at her, waiting for her response with caution.

"What's on your mind?" Linda looked at me worriedly.

"Huh? Nothing." I shook my head, trying to shake the image of my mother away only to have it cement deeper.

"Something is wrong. You can tell me anything." She pressed.

"I have just been thinking of my mum a lot today." I admitted glumly. My shoulders slumped with sadness. My eyes lowered to avoid her gaze.

"What about your mother were you thinking of?" Linda asked.

"Just her. How sweet she was and what she would think of me being here." My fingers entwined with each other. I picked nervously at the skin around my nail beds.

"She would be proud of you, sweetheart. She would happy you are getting the help you need." Linda's warm tone soothed my worried mind a little.

"Thank you, Linda." I smiled genuinely at her at her.
"Now, I have some good news for you." Linda rubbed her hands together.
"What news?" I was nervous. Maybe I was going home quicker than I thought.
"As your treatment is progressing well. I have allowed you to have some visitors tomorrow. So instead of your usual meditation, you will have family time."
"Who's visiting me?" I asked. I didn't want to see anyone.
"Your Aunt and Uncle."
"No. I don't want to see them. I will not see them, Linda." I refused, shaking my head from side to side. My hair whipping myself in the face.
"May I ask why not, Marty?" she asked.
"They put me here. I don't want to see them at all." My face went sour. My chest twisting with the savage response.
"Marty. They care about you. It might be good for you to see them and show them the progress you have made here." She attempted to urged me into wanting to see them. It wouldn't work.
"No." I stood my ground.
"It is entirely your choice. We just thought it would help speed up the process of you being here." Linda cocked an eyebrow.
"Fine." I said begrudgingly. I hated when she used that against me. The constant bargain for my freedom. I ground my teeth with displeasure.
"Good. Now let's talk about your mother." Linda grinned at me.

I went to bed that night with my head spinning. I didn't want to see them. I was still hurt by them doing this to me. They just dropped me at the first sign of sadness or any mental issue I had shown.
I tossed and turned all night on my hard bed. Acting as if I was asleep when the night nurse came to do the usual checks they did.

The moonlight shone through the venetian blinds on the window. The striped shadows covering the blanket as I curled up under them.
I was not looking forward to tomorrow in the slightest.

## Chapter Seventeen

Adam led me alone into the meeting hall. I had never been in there before. It was the same stark white with plastic floors and furniture as the rest of the centre. It looked just like the rest on thc centre. Other patients were having visits with their families. They all looked so cheerful. A part of me longed for that kind of happiness.
I looked around the other half of the bland room. My eyes darted to them the instant I moved.
John and Marion sat looking directly at me. John was holding Marion's hand and stroking it with his thumb for comfort.
I felt my anger bubble in my stomach as I stalked over to them, chewing my tongue so that I didn't burst out screeching at them in my seething rage.
Marion looked on the verge of tears as she got up to hug me as I reached the bare table.
She wrapped her short arms around my neck tightly. Her sweet perfume hitting my nose buried in her nest of curled raven hair. She buried her face in my messy hair that I hadn't been bothered to put into a style. I kept my hands by side. I wasn't going to hug her back. I hissed out a simmering breath as she tightened her grip.
John looked at me sadly. I could tell he wanted to hug me also, but he knew I would only do the same thing. His brown eyes gleaming with utter sadness, his heartbreak drawn over his tired face.

"We missed you, kid." Marion wiped a tear from her pale cheek as she sniffed more back.
"I'm fine." I kept my face neutral of any emotion.
"You are! You look well." Marion looked me over. She cupped my shoulders as she looked me over. Her eyes taking in all of me.
"Are they feeding you, kid?" John asked.
"Yes." I grunted.
"Doesn't look like it." He noted.
"Well, they do." I snapped quickly. Heat blazing through my cheeks, curling up to my ears.
"I'm glad they are, kid." He smiled and they sat back down at the table across from me.
I looked around the room before I sat and spotted Linda walking into the hall.
Taking my place from across from them, I sat down straight and looked at the pair I despised the most. They looked like they hadn't slept in weeks. They probably hadn't to be fair, but I didn't care. That was their cross to bear, not mine. I didn't lock me away here to rot.
"You look really well, sweetheart." Marion noted again.
"Thank you." I murmured.
"We missed you." Marion said sadly. Her blue eyes catching mine
I shrugged, not knowing what else to say. I glanced over at Linda who stood at the far wall watching on at my meeting, waiting for me to snap.
"We did this for you, kid. You do know that right?" John looked at me grievously. I felt a small pang of guilt in my chest, but my anger quickly overtook it.
"Did you though? Or was it just an easy of way of getting rid of your mentally screwed up niece?" I spat loudly, unable to control my pent-up anger. It flooded out of me like a raging fire.
"Martha!" Marion's tone bled her hurt by my outburst. I didn't care. I let it flood out of me.
Families at other tables turned their attention to me but I disregarded them. They didn't know me.

"If you had really cared about me, you would have helped me yourselves. Not lock me up in a looney bin. You let me go for years thinking that my father was alive. Letting me act all secretive and scared of my imaginary father. You knew he wasn't here and still you let me go on believing that he was out there. Out there watching me and living with me. Do you know how sick and twisted and cruel that is! Do you know how hard it was for me to make friends thinking that I had a father who I harboured as a dirty little secret?" I waved my arms as I stood from my seat.
"Marty. It's not like that at all." John tried to soothe me. His soft face dropped with grief.
"No! This is all your fault! You led me to believe that I was just fine how I was. That I was a normal kid. But I'm not and now you can't handle it! I am not your kid! I'm just some damaged orphan that you took in because you couldn't have a child of your own."
I looked at Marion. Tears had rained down her cheeks. Her black mascara had run down onto her lips. I had really hurt her. A small pang hit my stomach at the sight of her. My anger cooling to a simmer.
"All we ever did was love you, Martha. We gave everything we had to you. We gave up our lives for you to live a normal one. We didn't take you in because you were an orphan, we took you in because we loved you like our own." She pleaded.
"You took me in to right the wrongs you had with my mother, Marion. Just admit it." I gritted my teeth.
"No! That's not it at all." She gasped.
"Then why. Explain to me why you let me go on for twelve whole fucking years believing that my dad was real." I spat venomously.
"We tried to tell you." Marion looked at me with her eyes full of hurt.
"We did, Marty. We showed you the news, but you freaked out and went into this hole of manic depression. You came out of it believing that he was real, but we didn't want to break that happiness you had found.

You were happier than we had ever seen you before, kid." John explained.

"I was twelve!" I shouted, "I didn't know any better!"

I could see Linda making her way over to the table out of the corner of my eye. She placed a soothing hand on my arm, and I took a deep breath. I couldn't deal with being here any longer. I tried to summon my will to calm down but to no avail.

"I cannot even look at you both right now." I spat harshly again at the two of them.

I turned and hurried in my rage back to my room. I could hear Linda calling my name and apologising to them both profusely, but I didn't care. I wanted them behind me.

"Fuck off!" I called back, tears burning my eyes.

I hated them all.

## Chapter Eighteen

The week after my outburst was a long process. Linda had spent hours upon hours teaching me deal with my pent-up anger and encouraging me to forgive my family for leaving me here. It was a choice that I had given a lot of thought to, and I had slowly begun to realise that it wasn't their fault. They really did just want to help me. I knew that. I was just in a world of hurt. I cried in every session I had with Linda because of my guilt. I can only imagine what Marion must have felt. They really didn't deserve my harsh words and accusations. Not when they gave up their lives for me.

They came in on the following Saturday for my visiting hour. I didn't want to be alone with them again in case I had another episode, so I requested Linda to come along and sit with me. She accepted my offer happily.

"Hello, I am Linda McIntosh. I am Marty's therapist here." She greeted them and they each shook her hand. Linda pulled out the chair for me to sit down next to her leaving me with no option but to sit. She sat down next to me and crossed her hands on the table. My breathes were short and deep, just as Linda has taught me to do in stressful situations. A wave on panic washed over me. I picked at the pyjamas that I had worn on my first night here. They were the comfiest thing I had here.

"Now, Martha has come a long way in her short time here. She is still learning to deal with things, and I had hoped that her seeing her family would be beneficial for her last week, but I was wrong and that was my own misjudgement. So, for that I would like to formally apologise for her behaviour last week."

"Thank you." Marion accepted her apology. John nodded silently. His eyes never leaving her.

"Martha, would you like to say anything?" she asked, looking into my eyes. Her deep hazel ones urging me to apologise.

I felt the guilt from outburst bubbling in my body. I didn't know what to say. What if they hated me for my outburst?

"I'm so sorry. I don't know what came over me." I apologised. I took Aunt Marion's small cold hand in mine as she reached it across the table to me.

"It's okay, kid. You were just hurting." She smiled sadly.

"Honestly, I really didn't mean anything I said. I have hated myself for what I said." I explained softly.

"You don't need to explain yourself, love. We understand." John smiled at me warmly.

I had started to calm down further whilst Linda spoke to them about my advancement in my treatment. I would only be here for another two weeks by the sound of things. I wasn't ready to go home yet. Now that I was here, I felt as if I could never leave. I feared living in the outside world. I was terrified of people's judgement of me back home.

"Marty has made friends with a lovely girl here in the centre." Linda announced happily.

"Oh, really!" Marion said excitedly. She clapped with glee. The ghost of a smile flickered across my lips.

"Yes." I answered. It wasn't that big of a deal.

"Kresley has been a big help in Martha's treatment." Linda was particularly impressed with herself.

"That's wonderful news." John smiled excitedly. My gaze met his big brown eyes. He was genuinely happy for me.

"Yes, it really is. The two have formed a very close bond.

Maybe one day Kresley can come visit and you can visit her, Marty?" Linda suggested to me. I liked the idea of showing Kresley my café and my home. I couldn't wait to show her all my wildflowers. We could have girls' nights and be just like normal girls our age. It gave me hope to think that I could have a normal life after all of this madness.

"Of course! We would love to meet her." Marion gushed, her smile growing bigger. Her baby blue eyes crinkling with joy.

"And she can meet Eric." John suggested.

"What?" I choked out, shocked. Had they been talking to him?

"Eric, he would love to meet your friend!" John said.

"Eric is always asking us about you. He's always checking in twice a day at least. He really misses you." Marion assured me. She reached over the small table and squeezed my hand tightly. Her manicured nails pinching me. I winced in pain and withdrew my hand back.

"I thought he would have hated me after everything." I said as I rubbed my hand where I was pinched.

"Why would he hate you? Because he saw your tipping point? If he hated you for that Marty, then he is better off out of your life."

"He is only with me for pity." My self-doubt took over.

"He truly does love you, Marty." John assured me. "Trust me. I've seen it."

I smiled sadly. Things would never be the same between us. I felt the overwhelming urge to leave. The familiar rush of a panic attack brewing in my mind over me. My mind began to spin, and my breathing had become quick. Bile rose in my throat. My fingers pinched the soft flesh of my skin. Heat left my body.

"Linda, I need to leave." I began to shake vigorously.

"Are you okay, Marty?" Linda asked worriedly.

"I'm just getting overwhelmed now" I breathed. I looked into Linda's warm brown eyes. The golden flecks dancing in the fluorescent lights.

"Let's get you to your room, okay? Would you like to come into the centre and see Marty's room?" she asked John and Marion.

"We would love to." Marion cheered.

"Great!" Linda grabbed on to my arm. Helping my shaky body up. I held on tightly to Linda's arm as I rose. My feet began to tingle, and I felt like I could fall over at any moment.

We walked through the halls into the bed areas. Linda helped me stay calm as we walked through the corridor. She stood close to me, leading the way to my tiny room. I took my time counting to ten, counting each further step I had taken.

"Marty's room is just down here on the right." She waved a hand to my open door.

We walked into the plain room.

"An orange wall?" John questioned.

"It used to be a children's ward, but we thought Marty could use the colour as a mood booster." Linda admitted whilst feeling the hard wall. Her palm running over the smooth plaster.

"It's…cosy." Marion struggled to find words at my plain room. I could tell she hated the offending colour.

The clock on the wall read eleven fifty-five. Almost time for lunch.

"It appears visiting hour is almost up for today." Linda noted as she followed my gaze to the clock.

"Can we come back and visit you next week, Martin?" Marion asked me. Her voice hopeful.

"Of course, you can. I promise to be even better by then." I smiled and opened my arms for her. She hurried into them. She gave me a tight hug and patted my hair.

"You are the best you can be. I love you, always." She whispered,

"I love you always too." I whispered back.

She let me go for Uncle John gave me one of his famous bear hugs. His strong arms gripped me tightly as he held me above him. I let out a small giggle. He put me down gently on the lino floor and turned to Linda.
"Thank you for helping our girl, doctor" He shook her hand "We can't tell you how grateful we are for all of your help."
"There is no need at all to thank me. The pleasure is all mine. I am just happy to help this beautiful young woman in any way I can." She beamed as she cupped my shoulder gently.
I had begun to feel more normal than I had in a long time. It felt amazing. My panic lifting with each breath I took.

Linda led them down the hall and out of the centre. I hurried to the dining hall for my lunch. I felt ravenous after my meeting. I scoffed down the bland cheese sandwich and waited for Kresley who didn't come in today.
I began to get worried as I walked alone to the Arts hall. The room was empty apart from one person.
She was perched over her large dark portrait, deeply focused on her painting. Kresley looked up at me shocked.
"Oh, man. Did I miss lunch?" she whined.
"Yep." I sat next to her.
"Damn it." She slummed down into her seat beneath her.
I looked over at the painting. She was a very talented artist, but I couldn't make out the face just yet.
Kresley had already gotten my paint supplies and set it out for me, so I began to paint. I told her the names of all the wildflowers as I painted them. She listened happily as I painted them all for her. I even gave her my sheet when I was done.
"I love this. It's beautiful!" She beamed as I gave it to her. "You've got to sign it!"
"Why would I need to sign it?" I laughed.
"Every artist signs their work, Green."

I laughed and signed my signature small in the corner. Kresley tucked it safely to the side and focused back on her painting.
I dipped my thin brush into the water and began to paint more flowers. This time I painted a large pink rose for Marion. She had always loved roses but only the pink ones. She thought they smelled the sweetest.

## Chapter Nineteen

The days were beginning to pass quickly. It was already week four of my treatment and I had finally accepted that my father was dead.
Linda worked with me daily to show me how he was just a figment that I had made to cope with the fact that I had lost both parents so young. I felt sad for him and had since entered "the grieving process" as Linda called it. I was in the so-called last stage, acceptance.
It felt nice not to be held back by my grief anymore. It was a chance to start a new life. To leave my town. To travel. To do whatever I pleased. I didn't know what I wanted to do just yet, but I knew I wanted to something exciting. Something out of my comfort zone. I was finally ready to embrace the world. I decided that when I got out of the centre I would see if Charlotte would like to go out for a drink or do something 'normal'. I told myself that it couldn't hurt to ask, and I truly believed it.
I also truly believed Linda that it was all just a figment of my imagination and that I would confirm her words the moment I got home. A coping mechanism. Linda was very pleased with my progress as she came to my dorm on Saturday morning for our outside time before I got my family time.
"I am very proud of you, Marty. You have shown amazing progress in your treatment. You're almost ready to go home." She announced.

"Really? Do you think I am really ready to go back home?" I felt like I was glowing from the inside.

"Yes. Although, I'm not sure when. I need to sort out the finer details, but it won't be too much longer. If you need to stay longer though, you are welcome to extend the stay." She smiled at me happily.

"Thank you so much Linda." I hugged her tightly over the table.

"To celebrate, I managed to get you an extra half hour of family time today."

"You really are the best person I know, Doc." I chuckled.

"I know." She joked at me "Use the time you've got today wisely, okay?"

Linda led me to the meeting hall. I looked around for John and Marion, but I couldn't see them. The only person in the whole empty room was a tall boy with black hair. He grinned at me as I walked in through the door. I took a step back not realising who it was. He stood from his seat in the chair, and I fell back into Linda.

"Linda, who is that and why are they staring at me? Is this a new doctor? Am I seeing someone else now or…?" I asked in disbelief.

"Marty!" Linda cut me off. She laughed softly whilst steadying me on to my feet "How do you not recognise your own boyfriend. You joker!" she pinched my shoulder playfully.

"What?" I whispered. Shivers running rampant through my body.

"Your boyfriend." Linda chuckled.

"Eric." I exhaled with realisation. My heart sank. What was he doing here? He couldn't see me like this yet. I looked horrible. I was in my fuzzy jumper and blue jeans with my hair an unruly mess of waves.

"No, Linda!" I began to panic "I can't do this." I reached for her arm and gave it a nervous squeeze.

"Marty, it's okay. He really wanted to see you. This is a good chance to let him ease some of the self-doubt and worry you have been harbouring. Now just breathe like I taught you."

I began to breathe deeply as my eyes wandered over to where he sat.

Eric began walking up to where we were at the door. He looked so pleased to see me. I was happy to see him, but I was also worried. He was here to break up with me. I just knew it. The anxiety filled my body. My stomach turned itself in knots.

I froze on the spot as he approached me, my hands still around Linda's arm.

"Linda, please take me back to my room." I begged into her ear.

"Marty!" he said my name smoothly as he reached his strong arms out to hug me. I almost fell into them as I took shaky step forward from Linda. My fingers slipped down from her arm.

"I will leave you two to reacquaint." Linda whispered to me and left us to go to the coffee station at the wall. I watched as she walked away. Her curly red hair flowing behind her.

"Hello you." I breathed to Eric.

"I've missed you so much." He squeezed me tighter. His pine cologne intoxicating me. His head nestled into my freshly washed hair. My eyes fluttered shut.

"I missed you too." I nuzzled into his chest. His khaki green shirt soft against my cheek. His familiar warmth crept against my body.

"I am so sorry for doing this to you, Marty. I shouldn't have told them. I should have just let you cry. I should have just listened to you. I am so sorry, honey." his tone was full of guilt as he searched my face. I looked up at him and smiled. My gaze flicked to Linda who still had her back turned to us.

"You don't need to be sorry, Eric. I am where I needed to be." I had accepted their choice now. They really did just want what was best for me.

He let me go and led me to the table he was sitting at. A single plastic coffee cup sat on the sparklingly clean surface.

"So how have you been?" he asked, sitting across from me and taking a sip from his cup. He screwed up his face at the taste of the dark bitter drink. I couldn't wait to make my own coffees again.

"Well. I am an awful lot better now. Linda thinks I will be out of here pretty soon." I admitted. His bright blue eyes danced in the bright white light.

"They told me you will be out Wednesday." He smiled at me.

"Really?" I gasped happily. My hands cupped my mouth with shock.

"Yep. And I have some more good news for you, my love."

"What is it?" I asked, scared to know his answer. I began to scratch my thigh with anxiety. I glanced at Linda. She gave me a stern look and I stopped. I would be in trouble if I were to keep scratching myself, so I took a deep breath instead.

"I have been talking to your aunt and uncle and rather than you move back in with them. I am going to move in with you. Now I know we have only been together for a short time, but this past month has really sucked without you, Marty. I'll be honest. I missed you like crazy. I even messaged you every day."

"Really?"

"Of course!"

"I haven't checked my phone since I got here." I laughed.

"I want to be there for you. I want to be with you all the time. I want to help you anyway I can." He reached out for my hand, and I gave it to him. He grinned at me. His smile was infectious.

"Are you being serious about moving in?" I smiled back.

"One hundred percent." He grinned, squeezing my hand.

"Oh! I would love that, Eric!" I all but screamed.

"Perfect. Your aunt wants you to stay with them before hand to ease you back into normal life outside of here and by next Saturday hopefully we can move my stuff in and start a life together." Eric looked so happy with the plan they had created.

I was happy that he was happy. He made my heart race with pleasure.

I truly loved him with all of me. I loved him more than anything I had ever loved before. I imagined sitting in the field amongst the flowers with him, not doing anything but enjoying each other's company. It was my turn to live my own life and not listen to anyone else.

Eric updated me on how everything within the town was running and how Greg and Frank had organised a party at the café for me when I was home. According to Eric, they were so excited to see me again. Frank knew where I was, but Greg was told I was on a surprise holiday.

The town hadn't changed. Eric told me the police had searched my house to make sure I wasn't actually telling the truth about my father whilst I was here, but they couldn't find anything. Aunt Marion had gone in and cleaned everything up for me, so it was all nice and new when I went home. I was excited to go back home. I missed my own soft bed. I missed my wildflowers.

"I made a new friend here!" I blurted out.

"That's really awesome, Marty!" Eric cheered. "I'm proud of you."

"I know!" I was very pleased with myself.

"Who are they?" he asked intrigued.

"Kresley. She's helped me a lot here. She's like my own little feisty guardian angel" I said joyfully.

"That's sweet."

"I really mean little. She's like this tall." I gestured Kresley's tiny height beside me. Eric laughed deeply.

"I am so very proud of you, babe." He spoke. He had never called me babe before, but I liked it. A warm blush heated my cheeks. I grinned like a fool. My heart swelling.

I didn't realise how much I missed him until I had him within my grasp.

I asked Eric about how he went whilst I was gone and what happened with him.

He explained solemnly about how he just threw himself into his work because he felt so alone. He would call Marion every day to check if there were any updates. He told me about how Marion called him after my outburst and told him he would have to wait longer to see me and how it broke his heart and how he almost didn't believe it. He told me how he waited every single day to see if I had sent him a text, staring mindlessly at his phone until he would fall asleep holding it. He knew I couldn't send one back, but he couldn't help but check every chance he got. Charlotte had reached out to him to ask how I was doing as she hadn't seen me around and he lied to her and said I was away for a while on holiday. She offered to keep him company and he refused out of respect to me. He told me how ecstatic he was when it was finally his turn to visit me. He said he grinned the whole way here at thought of even seeing me again, listening to my favourite playlist the entirety of the drive.

My heart melted at this point. I blushed at every word he said. He was beautiful inside and out. It warmed my soul as he spoke about how much he missed me. It was this moment; I knew he loved me in the same way I loved him. The purest form of love I would ever experience.

Before I knew it, my time was up, and I had to go eat lunch.

"I'll see you real soon, okay?" Eric gave me a long hug goodbye. I wanted to kiss him, but it was too awkward with the staff and Linda in the hall watching on.

"I love you." I said softly. I had finally said it back to him. Fireworks filled my chest as I expressed it aloud.

"And I love you. God, I've missed you." He responded. Eric kissed me softly on the forehead. His clean-shaven chin cool against my blushing skin. Butterflies exploded in a flurry in my stomach. I reached up and pulled his lips to mine. He met them softly. I could feel that he wanted more but he knew he had to stop.
Eric left the hall with a young male nurse.
He smiled back at me as he walked out of the room. My heart racing after him.
I began to head down to the dining hall. I was excited to tell Kresley about my leaving and my surprise time with Eric. Linda smiled at me as I walked out the door.
"I told you! I knew you would be fine!" she called happily.
My feet fell hard as I dashed into the dining hall. The other patients looked at me puzzled with my urgency.
I sat down hard across from her.
Kresley sat beaming at me excitedly from the end of the table.
"I have news!" she announced.
"Me too!" I responded.
"I'm leaving on Tuesday!" she just about shouted.
"No way! I'm leaving Wednesday!" I shrieked back. My hands flapping around my face.
"No way!" she fluttered hers back.
"Yeah way!"
"That is amazing, Marty!" she gushed.
"And Eric is going to move into my house and live with me there!"
"Get out! No way!" her jaw dropped.
"I know." I felt like a kid in a candy store.
"I am so happy for you!" Kresley cooed.
"I'm happy for you too!"
Things were finally looking up and I couldn't wait to be out of here.

## Chapter Twenty

Soon enough, Tuesday rolled around I was allowed to spend my usual mediation hour with Kresley. I met her mother who looked just like her but with dyed purple hair rather than the faded aqua colour of Kresley's. She thanked me for looking after her daughter. It was sad to see Kresley leave but I had her mobile number, and I knew we would be friends outside of the centre. I would be lost without her now. I was glad I wasn't here without her for much longer, knowing I would struggle to cope on my own.
I went back to my room after my final ever arts and crafts session have finally finished. I had painted John and Marion a collection of Wildflowers in water colour. Adam had managed to find me a stray piece of twine so I could keep them all bound together.
I looked at the calendar hanging from the pin board. A tiny X drawn over each day I had been in here. I had circled the final day yet, my release. The third of May. The wildflowers back home would be in full autumn bloom by now. The summer months passing by colder than ever before. My body ached to lay amongst them and forget about the world for just a single brief moment. The sweet memory of their scent almost swelling in the room.

A large object under a soft brown fleece blanket Kresley had gifted me on my bed caught my gaze as I looked around my room. My fingers twitched as I pulled it off slowly. Scared of what else could be under there.

Under the blanket sat Kresley's portrait. Depicted was a girl painted in black and white surrounded by a thousand bright little wildflowers. It took me a moment to realise that the girl in the painting was me. I felt happy tears form in my eyes as I looked at the piece. It was truly beautiful. A note on the bed read *"Wildflowers in May."* Kresley's elegant handwriting swirled over the lined paper, a blatant disregard for the lines beneath. I grinned foolishly to myself and held the painting to my chest. I missed her terribly already. A soft hint of her patchouli perfume lingered on the canvas from the blanket. The fabric worn from years of use.

I packed my suitcase during quiet time and prepared for the next morning when I could finally go home. I hummed happily to myself as I placed my belongings back in my bag. A storm outside had brought a lot of patients panic as we ate our dinner, but I found it extremely soothing. It reminded me of home. I ate my creamy bland pasta and headed to my room for personal time.
I stared at the ceiling and for once in my life, I finally felt free. My father wasn't around to hold me back anymore, and I could start truly living my own life on my own terms. I could travel the world and see things I never thought I would ever have the chance to see. I had held on to the past for far too long now. I felt at ease with myself. I could finally live my life as a young woman and start a real life with my first love. In the house my mother had lived in with her first love. For once, I was excited to for the future. My chest fell softly with each breath I took. My mind had slowed, and my anxiety was at bay. For the first time in a long time, I felt genuinely at peace.
I curled up in my stiff bed for the last time and let the

sounds of the falling rain drift me off to sleep. I couldn't wait to be back home in my own soft plush bed. The weight of the world lifting from my exhausted shoulders.

The morning light filled my empty room, I arose happily. Today was my day.
The first day of my new life. No rules. My life to live the way I wanted it.
The warm water of the shower washed over me, willing all my doubt to flow down the drain with the dirty water. I brushed my hair and raked it up into a high sleek ponytail and brushed my teeth. I dressed in a pair of tight blue jeans with a light blue denim jacket. I practically floated to the dining hall for breakfast. I greeted Adam who served our breakfast on Wednesdays with a sweet smile and sat and ate my flavourless lumpy oatmeal, but I wouldn't let the lack of taste break my mood. I couldn't wait to make my own oatmeal back at home with berries and warming spices. It would be a vast improvement on the tasteless items they served here. The food had always been plain here. I wished they had made pumpkin risotto at least once. Gazing down at my now empty bowl, I decided that I would ask Eric to make it for me. He seemed like a more than capable cook. If not, I'd ask him to take me to eat it at least once a week. Just the first of my many little plans of getting out into the world as the new me. The new Marty. The brave Marty. The survivor Marty.
Linda met me back at my room after breakfast time had ended and let me know that John and Marion were outside waiting for me. She carried my yellow duffle bag holding my few possessions for me as I held my paintings for John and Marion and my portrait from Kresley close to my chest.
The sun shone warmly as we made our way out to the front entrance of the centre. The trees across the road waving at us as we stepped out. It felt like a dream to step outside the fortress of the centre. Excitement rolled over

me as I spotted John and Marion. They waved and took my yellow duffel bag from Linda.
Linda turned to me with a proud smile on her face.
I couldn't help myself.
I wrapped my arms around Linda and gave her a long hug goodbye. Her mature musky perfume pricked my nose. She stumbled on impact but wrapped her arms quickly around me.
"Thank you for all you have done for me, Linda. I can't tell you how much I appreciate everything you've taught me." I said into her neck as I bent down to hug her.
"You are more than welcome, sweetheart." Linda hugged me tightly back. "Look after yourself. And remember it's always okay to ask for help."
"I promise I will." I assured her.
I pulled out a painting from my stack. It was the first one I had done. My sprig of lavender. Linda blushed as I gave it to her. A proud smile creeped further across her face into a grin.
"As a thank you." I said, looking into her deep hazel eyes, the tiny flecks of gold dancing in the autumn sun.
"This is beautiful, Marty!" she looked up at me. Her soft eyes glowing with pride.
A small hand gripped the small of my back as I said my goodbyes to Linda. Marion crawled into the back seat and motioned for me to join her.
"Whose car is this?" I asked, noticing the new black hatchback that they had drove here.
I sat in the back with her. John explained that it was Marion's small black work car. Apparently, it was the same car that had brought me here, but I didn't notice the first time. It still had that new car scent lingering in the leather.
I smiled and watched happily out the window as we drove home in the rain. The feeling of peace still coursing through my body.

We arrived back at Marion and John's home two hours later. I was starving. John had run me a hot bath whilst I went to my old room to make myself at home. The room hadn't changed since I was seventeen. It was the same dull shade of white with a neatly made single bed in the right-hand corner of the room. Marion liked everything clean and fresh. I smiled as I placed the portrait on my desk opposite the bed on the left. I leant it gently against the wall so that I could see it at all times.

I noticed my phone was on charge and sat on the desk as well as a stack of brand-new novels. Linda must have given it to Marion before I was released. I unlocked it and read the messages.

There were ones from Frank and Greg, both wishing me well, the ones from Eric that he had sent every day and one from Kresley.

Kresley had sent me a photo of herself laying in her own bed, so I did the same and sent it back to her. My bed felt like a cloud compared to the one at the centre. I couldn't wait for my own bed at home.

John came in and sat next to me on the bed.

"You know what? I am so proud of you, kid." He wrapped an arm around my shoulders. I cuddled into his warm embrace.

"Thank you, Uncle John." I smiled at him.

"I would do anything for you kid, you know that right?" he placed his head on mine gently. His usual scent of wood filled the clean air.

"I know, John. And you know I would do the same for you right?" I looked up at him. He had his eyes closed, enjoying the moment.

"Now go have a bath before lunch is ready." He insisted.

"Oh, now that sounds nice." I purred as I left him alone in the room to head down to the large bathroom.

The water was hot as I lowered down softly into it. It's hot steam rising from my skin as I soaked. I had always loved a hot bath. John used to run them for me after I had been out in the rain on my way home from the café. He always said it was the best way to keep warm on a winter's day. I looked up at the white ceiling. The light danced in my eyes as I stared at the roof. I let my mind zone out. The silence felt calm over my ears.

"Lunch is ready!" Marion knocked on the polished clean door. I dried off and put on a fluffy warm robe over my underwear that Marion had put on the bench before I had even managed to get into the bathroom myself. I snuggled my face into the soft fleece fabric. Comfort flooding my body. The last tendril of warmth leaving my body.

We walked into the bright pristine kitchen. A large sandwich sat on the bench of the white stone kitchen counter. I ate it quickly, savouring every flavour it held. It was much better than the centre sandwiches and with not nearly as much mayonnaise as the centre painted on. Marion ordered me to get changed into a new pair of pyjamas she had brought me so she could wash the centre off my clothes.

The pastel green pyjamas were soft as I slid them over my skin. The peace filling my mind with utter bliss.

The tv played softly from the living room. I sat on the red suede couch and watched an old comedy movie curled up next to Marion after dinner whilst John tinkered around in his shed. Things felt as if they were finally back to normal.

## Chapter Twenty-One

I woke up the next morning and immediately checked my phone. I called Kresley and we spoke for an hour. She told me all about her apartment in the city and how much better she felt, and I told her felt the exact same way.
I ate my favourite honey oatmeal in the kitchen alone. I leant against the stone bench and inhaled my sweet concoction. After scarfing down the oatmeal, I went out into the lounge to join Marion who had her nose in a book. John was out for work, so I took a seat next to Marion on her big red couch and cuddled up to her. She put an arm around me as I laid into her. She smiled and snuggled her head back into mine. All whilst never taking her eyes off her novel. She had taken time of work to look after me. I was deeply grateful for the company. I scrolled through my phone for a while before heading to the shower. It felt amazing to wash my hair with proper products and to shave my legs. It felt so pleasing to be back to a normal way of life. Although, I did miss Linda.
I dressed and sat back on the couch with my own book next to Marion.
"They want to hold a party for you today." Marion broke the silence.
"Who does?"
"Frank and Greg." She shrugged as if it were nothing.
"Where?"
"Just at the café."
"Okay, when is it?" I was flattered.

"If it is too much for you, Marty. We don't have to go."
Marion's tone was reassuring at the least.
"It's okay. I want to go." I smiled.
"Well, go get your coat because it starts in fifteen minutes." Marion hurried me.
"Thanks for the extra time warning, Marion." I sneered playfully.
"Oh hush, Martin." She chuckled.
I walked to the long hallway and picked up my navy coat off the hook on the back of my bedroom door.
A shadow outside the window caught my attention.
I blinked and it was gone. I shook my head. I was just nervous about seeing my friends again.

Marion drove swiftly to the café. The morning sun heating the black seats of her car as she drove.
The café was full of people as we pulled up at the front.
"Jesus, they must have invited the whole town." Marion muttered.
A knot of anxiety rose in my throat. I swallowed it hard before entering the café.
"Welcome back, Marty!" Frank called.
"You're back, little love!" Greg boomed.
Patrons of the café looked around with curiosity as I stepped through the door. Marion's arm laced its way into mine. I accepted the gesture happily.
"How are you, my little love?" Greg said as he made his way over to me. His heavy feet scuffing against the blue tiles.
"I am absolutely fantastic, Greg." I beamed. Greg took me in his arms. His overpowering musky cologne burning my airways. I patted his back as he held me tight.
"That's great to hear!" he smiled. His moustache covering half of the cheeky grin.
"How have you been?" I asked him. Greg led me back to his usual table and waited for us to sit with him.

"Not too bad. Keeping an eye on the old man here. He went wild after you left kid. It was the weirdest thing." He rubbed his thick grey moustache as he glanced over at Frank behind the counter.
"How so?" I questioned him. My eyebrows furrowed with worry.
"He didn't ask for anyone to help him. He ran the whole show on his own. He made all these weird cakes and creations." Greg waved a hand in front of his wrinkled face. He ushered for us to sit down with him at his usual table.
"They weren't very good then?"
"Downright foul. Absolutely disgusting. Revolting" He grunted.
"Right." I drawled.
"I assume you were here every day then, Greg." Marion asked. Eyeing Greg's blue mug. She licked her glassy lips with hunger.
"Well, someone had to look after him." Greg huffed. He nodded his small head toward Frank behind the counter.
"I am going to get us a coffee." Marion stated as she stood up. Greg watched her leave before leaning over the table to me.
"They admitted you. Didn't they?" he whispered.
"What?" I whispered back.
"The put you in the looney bin."
"Greg!" I gaped "you can't call it that!"
"Bloody mongrels. You were doing just fine on your own. They tried to admit me when my wife died but I put up such a fight that they all abandoned me."
I laughed at his response.
"Well, I am an awful lot better now, Greg. Trust me." I assured him.
"Well, that's a positive thing, my darling. I'm glad you feel better." He smiled a lopsided smile. His moustache looked uneven with the motion.

Marion came back holding two blue mugs. The smell of coffee enticing my mouth. Saliva pooled as I ached for the bitter drink.
"One tall black for you and a chai for me." Marion pinched my cheek with her manicured fingers.
I scowled at her. My fingers rubbing my skin where the pain radiated.
"I hate when you do that." I narrowed my eyes at her.
"My wife used to do that." Greg grunted, eyeing Marion's hands.

"Really?" Marion questioned him cheerfully.
"Yep. She loved to do it to me. She knew how much I hated it, so she continued to do it. Even on her death bed the old bird gave me a tiny pinch.
I spat my coffee back into the mug as he finished his sentence. Marion eyed me as if to say, 'be quiet'. A smile spread across my face.
"You think that is funny, do you?" Greg raised his bushy eyebrows.
"It is a little." I admitted meekly.
"Well now, I might just start doing it to you from now on." He waved a bent finger at me. Light danced in his weary eyes.
I laughed at the gesture.
"I missed you terribly, Greg." I sighed.
"I missed you terribly too, my little love. This place truly isn't the same without you. It's far too dark and gloomy." His eyes clouded with admiration at me.
"Well, Greg. I think I will be here for a fair while longer yet." I reached out for his elderly hand. He took mine in his and gave it a tight squeeze.
"Don't get stuck here though, kid. There is a whole world out there to explore and a whole world of people to meet."
"I know. Thank you, Greg."
I took another sip of my hot coffee and listened to Greg talk to Marion about his old war stories.

Frank waved to me from behind the counter. Excusing myself quietly, I followed him into the back room.
His lanky arms engulfed me the moment I had my foot had stepped through the door.
"I am so glad you are back." He held my shoulders as he looked me in the eyes.
"I'm glad to be back." I smiled and placed my hands on his thin shoulders.
"That man has been driving me absolutely mental without you here." He pointed to Greg.
"He's alright. Just old." I chuckled with a half-hearted shrug.
"Old and senile." He scoffed.
My eyes wandered to my surroundings in a place so familiar yet so foreign.
Frank had reorganised the storeroom. Things weren't in their usual place. It would take a long while to figure where he had moved everything to. My breathing coming to ten.
"When are you ready to come back?" Frank asked quickly.
"What do you mean?" I cocked an eyebrow.
"When would you like to come back to work?" he asked again.
"Whenever you would like me to." I let go of his shoulders gingerly.
"Would Monday work?"
"That sounds absolutely perfect to me." I couldn't wait to be back at work and back into a normal routine.
"Perfect. Nine am." He nodded.
"Nine am." I repeated, mimicking his nod to me.
Frank pulled me toward him. He wrapped his thin arms over me once more.
"You are just as strong as your mother. Never forget that." He spoke. His head resting on my shoulder. He patted my back roughly. I hugged him back silently.
I smiled as I let him go. He grinned back at me and gestured as if he was pushing me away from him.
I laughed as I walked back out to the front of the café.

A man walked by the window. His scruffy demeanour catching my attention. He glanced in the window at me. My heart sank as I stepped back with fear. I blinked and he was gone. Vanished into thin air.

"It was no one. You're fine." I whispered to reassure myself. I was just overwhelmed by all of the people.

I sat back down across from Greg. The blood had drained from my face in fear.

"Are you okay, Marty?" Marion asked, placing down her now empty mug. The smell of cinnamon tainting her breath.

"Of course." I nodded with a forced smile. I shook my head. "I'm fine."

## Chapter Twenty-Two

The days passed quickly but I didn't see Eric. He was extremely busy with work and packing for our big move. It hurt to know that he was too busy for me, but he assured me every day that soon he would be all mine, I was quite anxious, but I was also very excited about it all. The sense of knowing what I was going to do with my life felt fantastic.

I woke up on Saturday bursting with energy. I got up and showered in a scolding hot shower. My favourite song played from my phone, and I sang my heart out along to it as the water fell against my already burning skin.

I ate my favourite hot oatmeal for breakfast and packed my things back into the yellow bag. John and Marion were both gone before I was up so I sat on the couch and waited for them both to arrive before they could drive me back to my home. The rattle of an old engine echoed outside. I stood and opened the lace curtains. There she was. My big red truck.

John let me drive home alone so that the two of them could go over to help Eric pack his things. I drove slowly home taking in the scenery. It was a sunny day and the light bounced off the vibrant green trees as I drove under them. Leaves twirled, falling with a dance onto the open road.

The house looked the exact same as it was when I had left. No sign of anyone living there at all.

My heart began to pound with nerves. My mind raced with the thought of oncoming danger.

"He's not there, Marty. He isn't here anymore..." I reassured myself, trailing off as I drew in a deep breath. I gulped back the lump in my throat as I looked at the front door.

I climbed out of the warm car and headed into the house. The clouds had formed overhead. Their heavy downpour imminent.

I opened the old front door. It creaked as it swung back. The scent of dust raced outside with the motion. I crinkled my nose at the smell of it. No one had been here in a while.

The emerald vase sat empty at the entry table. I hurriedly threw my bag onto the plush couch and went out to the field next door. I had waited so long for this moment.

I ran my hands over the wildflowers. Their soft petals helping me feel at peace. The colours danced together in the breeze as their sweet smell swirled in the damp air. I lowered myself to finally lay amongst them. The dream was nothing compared to the reality.

Time ticked slowly around me until I gently plucked a bunch of random blooms that had caught my eye. Smiling as a stray ray of light hit them directly. The rain holding back long enough for me to embrace my happy place.

They sat nicely in the vase as I placed them down into it. The green glass glistening in the streaming afternoon sun. I gathered my strength before carrying my heavy suitcase up to my room.

I unpacked the contents and hung up my portrait over my own bed. A constant reminder of Kresley and how much she had helped me grow as a person. I couldn't thank her enough for helping me through the whole strange experience at the centre.

The sun continued to shine through the clouds and into my room as I put my belongings away into my wardrobe.

"Hi, Mum." I said to the sun light. I knew she was around me when the sun was out. It was like her way of

comforting me.
My fingers danced in the warmth from the light.
I headed downstairs and put the kettle on. My stomach rumbled at the thought of a cup of black tea. I drank my tea and called Kresley. She spoke for an hour or so and we planned for her to come visit in two weeks. I felt like your average twenty-three-year-old girl. Completely normal and full of life.
I stood happily and went to the staircase, staring at the non-existent outline. My fingers tracing where the door to Dad's secret room could have been. There was never a cupboard under them let alone a door. I traced them to feel if there was anything only to find nothing. It was just an illusion. My fingertips feeling nothing but the smooth fading wallpaper.
"He's not here. He isn't real." I assured myself.
Taking several deep breaths, I sat back on the couch and took in the house to myself.
Eric would be here in just over an hour. I had an hour of the house left to myself. My last hour alone.
The sun had begun to go behind clouds again. It was going to rain tonight, that I was certain about. I turned the heater on to make sure I stayed warm and so that it was nice and cosy for when the others arrived. I went to look out the large front window, staring at the storm rolling over.
I ran my hands over the thick linen curtains. Flecks of dust began raining down from my gentle touch.
A floorboard creaked behind me. I didn't bother to turn around. It was just the house settling.
It creaked again.
This time gaining my full attention. I turned to see nothing. I looked back at the kitchen. My heart jumped rapidly with the sudden noise. My senses were on full alert. Waiting for the next sound.
Nothing was there.

I turned back to the window and continued to wait for them. I admired the trees blowing softly in the breeze. The floor creaked again, and I decided to investigate. My heart raced and my breath caught in my lungs as I took a step toward the kitchen.

"Hello?" my voice crackled as I called out.

I walked cautiously to the kitchen. I walked as silently as I could, peering my head around the corner of the archway and into the kitchen.

No one was there. Just the same empty kitchen as always. I exhaled with relief. My body relaxing as I walked back to the window. I could feel my nerves stirring in my stomach whilst I waited for them.

A brown lump caught my attention from the corner of my gaze. I turned to look at the mantel piece.

There sat my carved bookends. John must have brought them over for me whilst I was away.

"Come on." I said to myself in an effort to hurry everyone up. I didn't want to be alone any longer than I had to be. The storm gathered overhead a clap of thunder boomed through the silent forest. Paranoia set in.

The roar of an engine caught my attention. I turned my gaze to the driveway where Eric's silver sports car rolled up the driveway with John and Marion not far behind.

I opened the door for them as they carried the large cardboard boxes in.

I wasn't allowed to help. John didn't want me 'exerting myself' as he put it. They carried each box into the living room and put them neatly in the archway by the kitchen. Eric's scent lingering on each box.

"There's not a real lot is there?" I noted seeing how little Eric brought in.

"I don't need a lot." He shrugged it off.

"Fair enough." I mumbled.

"What are you two going to do tonight?" Marion asked.

"Unpack and then just relaxing with a movie sounds nice." Eric smiled. I was itching to have Eric to myself. To have his arms around me and his lips on mine.

"Oh, now relaxing sounds amazing." Marion sighed tiredly. The exhaustion lining her face.

"Well now, love. Let's go home and let them settle in so that *you* may relax." John cupped Marion's shoulders in his big hands and kissed the top of her head lightly. Her hair a mess from moving.

"Okay. Goodnight, guys. Marty, I'll be over sometime tomorrow for a little check in."

"No worries. I'll see you then." I gave her a hug goodbye before doing the same to John.

I watched as they drove away. Eric's strong arms snaked around my waist as he pulled me back closer to him. His breath warm on my neck as he kissed my cold skin.

"Welcome to our forever." He whispered.

"Welcome." I grinned, embracing his affection.

His hands slipped down to my thighs, and he took a step back. I spun to face him.

"Do you want to help me unpack?" he asked.

"Of course." I nodded.

I opened the first box of a stack. The cardboard ripping loudly as I wrenched it open. Inside sat a small teddy bear staring at me. I was taken aback. What on earth was that? I couldn't help but let out a small laugh.

I lifted it up slowly to inspect it. It had green velvet fur with beady black eyes. One foot was rather thread bare and the stomach was missing fur in some places. The soft toy clearly older than I was.

"I knew you would find him before I could." Eric reached for the small bear with an embarrassed look on his face

"What is it?" I asked, handing it to him quickly as if it would crumble in seconds.

"My teddy bear."

"Right." I drawled. A smile burst across my face.

"What?" he laughed.

"I have just never heard of anyone really having a teddy bear into their twenties. That's all." I chuckled.

"Is that right, Martha May?" he cocked an eyebrow.

"Yep." I said defiantly. "And that is not my name."

"Well in that case…" Eric said as he lunged playfully toward me. I stepped back and fell directly on the plush couch. I threw the bear back over to the boxes as my body tumbled backwards.

Eric stood over me, placing his hands above my shoulders so I couldn't move. My heart began to race as his lips got closer to mine. Their touch bringing a sweet rush of ecstasy through my body. My mind thinking of nothing but how he amazing tasted. Sparks flew through my body. It was the first time I actually had kissed him in months, not just a light peck. He pushed me back hungrily. His lips hard against mine, longing for more.

His hands moved slowly to cup my face and I felt my hands reach up to pull him down to me.

"Should we take this upstairs?" he asked, breaking the blissful moment.

"Take what?" I asked seductively, wanting more of his touch.

"My teddy bear, Marty!" he laughed "Get your mind out of the gutter." I rolled my eyes at his joke and laughed.

"You are just so funny, Eric." I pulled a face, lightly tapping his bicep.

"Hey! None of that!" he waved the small green toy at me. I laughed deeply at his fascination with the bear.

"Where did you even get that?" I asked.

"My mother got it for me before I was even born. I've had him ever since." He shrugged happily.

"That's actually really sweet." I admitted.

"Yeah, I think so." Eric looked down at the bear and fumbled its red silk bowtie between his fingers.

I knew it was going to be a long night.

## Chapter Twenty-Three

I woke up the next morning to the sound of Eric's beeping alarm ringing loudly in my ears.
We had decided to stay in my room for now until I had enough courage to clean out my parent's master bedroom. Although they weren't here anymore, a part of me was still fearful of what I would find.
Eric groaned sadly as he turned the alarm off, rolling over gently to face me. His eyes squeezed shut as the sun blazed through the open window.
"How do you sleep with that?" he grunted and pointed a limp hand at the window.
"It's beautiful. I love looking at the sunrise each morning." I looked out at the morning field. The flowers beginning to open with the warming light of the sun. The storm had cleared overnight, and everything looked so luscious, green and full of life. But in the distance the sun was slowly going behind a looming storm cloud. Birds chirped their morning song as they danced and fluttered their way through the open field, dancing in the remaining light.
It was going to be another wet night.
"Nothing on this planet will ever be as beautiful as you." Eric sat up and kissed my cheek softly.
 My mouth curled into a small smile, blood rushing to my face.
"Are you hungry?" he asked sleepily.

"I can eat." I shrugged. Looking at his tired blue eyes. His bed hair flopped all over his face.

"Good. You stay here." He ordered. His tall frame hoisting itself out of the bed gracefully.

"I can help." I tried to get out of bed with him.

"No, you stay up here and rest. I will call you when it's done." He leaned over the bed and pulled my chin to his with a single finger. His mouth softly grazed mine.

I watched him as he left. A wave of happy bliss enveloped me as I laid back on my pillows, stifling my excited squeal brought on from the overwhelming joy I was experiencing. It was hard to imagine this was my life now. Years of being alone, now filled with love and devotion. If only my younger self could see me now.

A floorboard groaned in the hallway catching my attention. Blood froze beneath my skin. I listened to see if it creaked again.

Nothing.

I swung my legs out of bed quickly and hurried downstairs. My cold feet padded loudly as I raced down the stairs.

"Eric?" I called.

"I thought I told you to wait upstairs until I was done." He turned away from the stove and wove the metal spatula at me.

"I heard a weird noise. I didn't want to be up there alone any longer." I swallowed hard. My teeth biting hard into my bottom lip as I nibbled with panic. I clutched a dining chair for support. My breathing short and shallow.

"Are you okay?" he asked. His face reading mine, eyes darting all over my trembling form.

"I'm fine. Just learning to cope." I swallowed hard again. Hoping my fear would go with it.

"Good. Now sit." He waved the metal tool toward my chair at the table. I sat down on the wooden seat and watched as Eric flipped pancakes. His flips graceful and fluid as if he had been doing it for years.

When he was done. Eric placed the dish in front of me.

The pancakes flooded under a river of maple syrup with a mixture of red berries on top. Drowning in the thick amber liquid. I didn't really like maple syrup, but I would eat it for Eric's sake.
"Well dig in." he smiled as he sat across from me.

I picked up my knife and fork in my shaky hands. The knife sliced straight through the pancake stack, syrup pouring out from the wound. I gulped back my disgust and ate the mouthful. The sweet sauce sticking to my mouth as I chewed it. I tried my best to conceal my distaste.
"Are they good?" Eric asked, swallowing his mouthful and chasing with a cup of orange juice.
"Yep" I said stiffly "Very nice."
"I'm glad!" he beamed proudly.
We ate in silence. Eric finished his entire stack before I could even finish one small pancake. He waited patiently as I finished the last of the sickly-sweet breakfast slowly. I wasn't going to let him see me dislike his first meal he had prepared for me in his new home.
A loud buzzing filled the silent room. The phone vibrated harshly against the wooden table.
"Hello, Eric speaking." He answered the phone professionally.
Eric walked out onto the back porch, closing the door behind him.
I looked down at my empty plate with a sigh. The scene reminded me of dad.
"He was never really here, Marty. You know that." I reassured myself with another sigh.
My hands stuck to the plates as I ran hot water over them. The syrup sticking as I scrubbed it off with the sponge. By the time I was done, Eric had come back inside.
"I have to go in to work for a bit. Will you be okay here on your own?" he asked frantically.
"Of course, I have done it for years remember. Is everything okay?" I responded worriedly.

"Just work stuff." His voice echoed as he raced up stairs. The pump outside hummed to life as Eric turned the taps in the bathroom on.
I was wiping down the table when he raced back downstairs.
"I'll be home soon, okay?" he called from the front door.
"Will you be here after?"
"Where else would I go?" I laughed as he slammed the front door behind him. His sports car roaring to life as he sped into town.
My mind raced as I hurried to watch him drive off. I wished he wouldn't speed. I didn't want anything bad to happen to him.
With Eric being gone for a fair while, I decided to shower and read a new book I had started from the pile john had left me. I slipped on a pair of black lounge pants and sat on the couch to tie my shoes, planning to go into the field before another storm rolled over.
A loud creaking noise broke my concentration as I bent down to tie my shoe.
I ignored it and finished tying the tight bow.
Another creak came from the kitchen. This time louder.
My heart raced as I got up to see what would be making the noise.
I peeked my head through the archway slowly.

## Chapter Twenty - Four

"There is no one here, Marty." I assured myself with a whisper. My heartbeat ricocheting against my chest.
The wind howled through the open kitchen window. A storm was rolling over.
I nibbled at my bottom lip as I slammed the window shut. The creaking stopped.
"See! It was just the house settling." I smiled in an attempt to calm my nerves that ran wild through my body.
Making my way to laundry, I noticed the hamper had some clothes it. Grateful for something to do, I stuck them in the washing machine and began the quick cycle. The thought of warm water filling my body with the need to be under hot water. I didn't have a bath here, but I did have a shower. It would have to do.
It felt as if I was floating on a cloud as I padded lightly upstairs. My hand fumbled for the brass door handle before swinging open. The old hinges groaned with the sudden movement.
I looked at my face in the small mirror. Years of fear that had once lined my face had disappeared. A new woman stood before me, a strong brave independent woman, and I swore I would never let her go. I grinned at my reflection. The face smiling back at me. A wave of pure glee ran

through my body. My skin tingled with the unusual sensation.

The water ran hot over my smooth skin. Steam danced from the running tap as it cascaded over my body. I felt myself relaxing even further. My hands danced their way through my wet hair, pushing the lavender product all over my head. The scent intoxicating me with a sense of normality. My sense of time falling with the bubbles of shampoo down the drain.

I wrapped a towel around myself after turning the water off. My skin burnt red from the steaming shower. A cold chill ran over my body.

I hurried into my bedroom to get dressed. I needed warmth.

The sun outside had faded and the cloud that had loomed had finally taken over. The deep grey sky making the day feel later than it was. My mind wandered to Eric. A small pang of nerves hit my stomach. I hoped he was okay.

I walked toward my wardrobe in the corner, oblivious to any sounds that the house was making.

I was heavily focused on what I would wear to keep warm. A warm pair of pants and a thick jumper should suffice. It was freezing in the house. The icy wind howling around the yard.

"Well, now that is a sight for sore eyes." Eric's deep voice sent a wave of panic through my body. I clenched my towel tighter against myself as I panted for the breath he had stolen. My eyes snapped wide open, and I turned to face him. Heart hammering deep inside my chest.

"You scared the life out of me!" I gasped. Panic flowed through my body, shaking me to the core.

"I'm sorry." He said softly, running his soft fingers over my cheeks.

"It's okay." I mumbled. The beat of my heart slowing slightly with his touch.

"You smell amazing." Eric moaned in my hair. A deep laugh left my mouth.

"And people think *I* am the strange one."

"*I* am not the strange one, Martha." He joked.
"Don't call me that, Eric. I'm not over sixty." I glared into his eyes. My angered reflection glistening in their soft blue.
"You really don't like being called that do you?" he laughed lightly. I puffed and turned back to my dresser. I grabbed a pair of plain underwear and slid them on under the towel.
I could feel Eric's stare burning into me as I dressed. I pulled a pair of comfortable pants from the dressers bottom drawer and threw them on top of it. My fingers ran over my various vintage t-shirts. Stopping on a pale green one. I took a deep breath. I prepared myself and dropped the thick towel from my body. I was facing away from Eric which brought a slight sense of comfort whilst I slid the soft worn cotton over my head. My fingers pulled it tightly down before reaching for the pants I had selected. Eric's delicate grasp around my waist brought a smile to my face.
"What was that for?" he whispered in my ear as he kicked my towel into the corner of the room.
"What was what for?" I whispered softly back.
"You know what." He hissed softly into my ear.
"Teach you not to stare at me." I shrugged.
"Well, it's hard when the one you're looking at is as captivating as you." He breathed in my ear. His strong body pressed against my back. My heart began to pound loudly in my ears. Eric's lips softly grazed my neck. The smooth skin sending a shiver up my spine.
"I feel the same way every time I look at you." I spoke softly. My lips aching to feel his against mine. I could feel him smile against my cheek.
"Shall I go prepare us a lunch, my lady?"
"We didn't have breakfast that long ago."
"It was over three hours ago."

"Was it?" I gasped. I didn't think I had spent that long in the shower. The water bill was going to be high next month.
"Yes." He laughed. His hands twitched before turning me to face him. My body still pressed firmly up against his. The warmth from his skin tingling against my cold ones. Goosebumps had begun to form on my freezing legs.
"I should put pants on." I muttered.
"I beg to differ." Eric shrugged but let me go. I hurried to put the pants on, embracing the warmth they brought. I slid on an old sweatshirt and made my way back to Eric. He stood with his head tilted, his gaze locked on me. The blush on his pale skin flooding a fierce rose colour into a snow-white face.
"Now, now. It's freezing. We need to put the heat on." I shivered. Thunder cracked loudly outside the window. Rain began to fall lightly against the window. Streaks of diamond like water lined the clear glass. I jumped. Startled by the loud noise.
"Come on then." Eric's hand took mine as he led me downstairs.
I followed him back down to the living room.
"Sit." He ordered, pointing at the soft couch. I obeyed and sat down in the centre. Eric lifted the brown blanket Kresley had gifted me that was swung over the back of the couch and threw it over me. His hands gentle as he slowly tucked the blanket under my body. He smiled to himself as he did. He handed me a book and nodded for me to begin reading.
My fingers traced the outline of the brand-new book. He must have just brought it for me. I looked at the front cover. It was blank. No title. Just black leather with a gold trim.
"Weird." I mumbled.
I cautiously opened the cover, curious as to what was inside. The title read "Wildflowers and their many uses." I

blushed furiously as my eyes reread the title. A pang of guilt hit my heart. I didn't deserve Eric. I knew it in my core.

"I thought you would like it." Eric kissed my forehead as he slipped a small teacup into my hands in place of the book. I smiled, warmth filling my face.

"Thank you, Eric. You really didn't have to get me anything." I smiled up at him. He lifted my legs upward and sat down on the couch beside me. I slowly lowered my legs onto him. The warmth of my legs heating his cold dress pants.

His pale skin glistened in the dim light from the window outside. The smell of rain lingering in the thin crisp air. Rain padded softly outside.

I stared at the world beyond the window, raising the small teacup to my lips. The hot liquid steaming into my nose. Hot with no sugar. Just the way I liked it. A large smile broke across my face as the amber liquid skimmed against my lips. Eric's gaze had followed mine to the forest outside. My eyes slowly drifted to where he sat, admiring him.

His soft black hair curling with a new length. He had not cut it since before I had gone into the centre. The longer look really suited him. His pale baby blue eyes shining in the dim afternoon light. He looked tired. But he also looked happy. I watched as a smile crept across his lips.

"It's rude to stare." He teased. His focus now back on me.

"Sorry." I mumbled awkwardly. A feeling of anxiety rushed to my head.

"I'm kidding, Marty." Eric laughed lightly. His soft palm grazed my leg.

"Good. I was just admiring how beautiful you were." I breathed over the rim of my cup.

"I do the same every time I am near you. I just can't take my eyes off you." He moved his hand over my leg concealed by the fuzzy blanket and gave it a tight squeeze.

A hot flush crept across my cheeks. Rain began to fall heavier outside, and the wind had begun to howl loudly around the old house.

"Should I light the fire?" I asked, looking over to the empty fireplace. I craved the earthy warmth it brought.

"I will do it. You stay right there." Eric ordered, shuffling out from under me.

"Let me help." I chuckled.

"Nope." He said sternly.

"Alright boss man." I offered a dramatic salute before returning to my book. It was nice to have someone else care for me for once.

## Chapter Twenty-Five

The heavy rain continued to pour down well into the night, but it didn't stop the sun coming out in full force for sunrise. The wind had settled to a soft breeze and the trees no longer shook with force.
Heavy footsteps raced toward the bedroom. Panic took over my body. I curled myself up into my corner of the bed and braced for the impact, scared of who it may be.
"Happy Friday!" Eric shouted cheerfully as he leapt onto the bed in front of me.
"You scared the life out of me!" I hissed, raising myself from the ball I had curled myself into. My heart beating fast against my chest.
"I am terribly sorry, Marty. But Frank has called to ask if you would like to come back to work today instead of Monday." He grinned at me with his perfect smile.
"Really?" I gasped. I was excited about the concept of working again but I was also terrified of people seeing me back working at the café.
"Of course."
I smiled and pushed past Eric to get my uniform hanging from the wardrobe. The thrill of being useful again ran rampant through my body.

"Welcome home, Miss Marty!" Frank called. I had barely

stepped over the threshold when he noticed me.
"Thanks Frankie!" I called back.
It was nine am and the café was eerily silent. The sweet smell of coffee coating the cool morning air.
"How are you feeling?" Frank materialised from the back storeroom.
"I am pretty good actually." I admitted.
"I am happy to hear that. You remember what to do?" he joked.
I poked my tongue out at him as I slipped my apron around my waist. The soft blue linen hugging my body. I breathed in heavily, embracing the normality.
"Much better." I sighed softly.
"I bet." Frank chuckled to himself as he left me to man the front counter.
The café was too quiet without the radio, so I turned that on first. People began to fill the café and I served each and every one with ease. My anxiety contained in the back of mind. I wasn't going to let it get the best of me today.
"Hey, Marty!" a familiar bubbly voice called. I turned too quickly to face her. My balance failing me. My hand gripped the counter for support.
"Hey, Charlotte." I breathed, choking for air after my sudden shock.
"I am so sorry. I didn't mean to startle you!" She apologised quickly, her body leaning against the counter as she bent to grip my shoulder comfortingly.
"It's all good. What can I get you?" the anxiety I had contained slowly crept out.
"Well, I was actually here to see what you were doing tomorrow." She shrugged her perfect slender shoulders. Her long straight blonde hair cascading around them with the motion.
"Oh. I- nothing actually. Why's that?" I stuttered. My eyes wide with panic.
"Would you like to have a girl's night, just me and you?" her purple painted nails tapped on the counter.

"I'd love that." I smiled small, nervous to say anything else.

"Perfect!" Charlotte bubbled "I can come over to yours if you like and we can watch a movie?"

"I'd love that." My smile spread wide against my face.

"Text me your address and I'll be there say seven o'clock." She grinned. Her brown eyes gleaming with joy. Her manicured nails sliding her number scrawled on a scrap piece over to me.

"Can do." I tried my hardest to sound like I wasn't ecstatic about having a friend I could speak to.

## Chapter Twenty - Six

"That's great Marty!" Eric beamed as I told him the news about Charlotte and me.
"I know." I shrugged happily.
I had come home to Eric cooking dinner for our night with John and Marion. He had finished early and had bet me home. With the café being as hectic as it was, it was four before I could even hang up my apron.
"Would you mind if I went to the city to see my family then?" Eric asked.
"No. Of course not!" I gushed, concerned as to why he had to ask my permission.
"Good." He beamed again, drawing me into his warm arms. His strong embrace comforting my aching body.
"What will you do there?" I asked. Resting my chin on his firm chest as I looked up at him.
"I need to see my family. I have to tell them all about this amazing girl I met and how beautiful she is and how I now get to call her my girlfriend." His lips fell softly onto the top of my head.
"Oh, hush you." I giggled into him. His familiar soft spiced scent filling my nose with pleasure.
"Go get changed. You reek of coffee and fondant." Eric playfully pushed me away.
"Yes, sir!" I raised my hand into a salute and left Eric alone in the kitchen.

I washed quickly in the shower before making my way back down the stairs.

The back of Eric's head was visible on the couch. He sat straight at all times, always with perfect posture.

His soft black hair beginning to drape over the plush couch.

"What are you doing?" I asked.

Eric jumped. Startled by my question.

"Nothing." He said quickly. I was confused by his answer. What was he hiding?

"Didn't sound like nothing."

"Honestly, I was doing nothing. I just deep in my thoughts, that's all." He turned his body to face me as I made my way to the couch where he sat and put myself down next to him. The soft brown blanket was draped over his legs more for comfort than warmth. The woodfire crackled loudly. Heat racing out from the burning wood.

"What were you thinking about?" I asked, reaching my fingers out to brush a stray curl from his face.

"It's nothing." He said hurriedly.

"Come on. Dish the goss." I chuckled.

"Well little miss nosey. If you really want to know you're going to have to make me tell you." His eyes alert, trying to read if I was interested in his little game.

"And what does that entail?" I played along. A smirk crept across his lips.

"Hmm." He hummed.

A wave of confidence caught me off guard. I was too curious to play his game. I needed to show him that I wasn't some little scared girl like everyone thought I was. I needed to prove I was stronger than he gave me credit for and more open to new things. I took a deep breath in and leapt onto his lap, straddling his thighs. I moved myself closer to him. My body against his as I leant forward and placed my lips against his soft mouth. Eric tensed from the sudden impact but softened the moment he realised what I had done. He pushed his body against mine harder and his

lips firmly into mine. His delicate hands snaked their way up my back. I ran my fingers through his hair. Our lips broke apart for air, I ached for more of his touch. Now was my chance.
"So, what were you thinking about?" I whispered into his ear.
"I was thinking about how I am going to marry you someday." He breathed softly.
"What?" I gasped.
"I am going to marry you one day, Marty." He pressed, his soft blue eyes searching mine with panic.
A giant grin swept across my face. Blood flooded my cheeks with warmth.
"You're a goose." I teased. My heart raced with happiness as butterflies danced in my stomach. The thought of spending every day with Eric for the rest of my life was like a dream I had dreamt of for so long finally coming to fruition. I leant back down and kissed him softly. He kissed back. Fireworks erupted within my body. Sparks clouded my mind. I knew deep in my bones that this was my true love.
I pulled myself back and smiled at Eric. His soft hands holding my back tightly.
"I love you." I said without thinking.
"I love you more." Eric responded, his cheeks burning a deep red with blush.
Gravel crunched on the driveway to the house. John's white work truck pulled up right out the front of the porch.
"They're early." Eric noted.
"I wonder what for?" I mumbled. The clock on the wall read 5:34. Dinner wasn't until 6:30.
A knock on the door was enough to push me off Eric's lap. I straightened my pants before heading to the door. The door flew open before I could even reach the threshold.
"Marty?" Marion called, excitement tainting her serious tone.
"Hi!" I welcomed them. The two of them were both wearing smug grins.

Panic raised in my chest.
"What's going on?" I cocked an eyebrow.
"Let's go sit as a family. Come on, Eric." John waved at Eric. He stood from the couch and shook John's hand. Marion led us into the kitchen. Her beige coat swaying behind her as she bounced to the kitchen.
I sat down hesitantly into my usual seat at the table. Eric stood next to me with a comforting hand on my shoulder. John reflected with Marion as she sat down across from me.
"Marty." Marion bubbled.
"Yes, Maz?" I laughed nervously. My chest constricting with the growing panic.
"I don't think I will be drinking any wine tonight."
"What? You never turn down a wine. Is everything okay?" I asked confusedly. I looked up at Eric to see if he knew what was going on, but he looked just as puzzled as I was, if not more.
Marion's dainty hand reached inside on of her jackets inner pockets and pulled out a thin white envelope. She slid it across the table to me. her hands shaking with the motion. John beamed as he gripped Marion's shoulder supportively.
I reached down hesitantly to the envelope. Silently wishing for it not to be from the centre.
My fingers opened the envelope carefully as to not rip it. the envelope felt weightless as I opened it up fully, dragging the contents out slowly. There was nothing but a blank piece of card.
"What is this?" I laughed.
"Turn it around silly!" Marion chuckled loudly.
I turned the piece of card over. A loud gasp left my mouth as it fell open in shock. Tears burnt at my eyes. My heartbeat soared against my rib cage.
The picture of the ultrasound had rendered me speechless.
"No!" I gasped again.
Marion nodded with tears filling her big brown eyes. My own tears of happiness begun to fall onto my cheeks. I

leapt from my spot, sending Eric backward. John wrapped his arms around me.
"Congratulations!" I said excitedly.
Marion stood and wrapped her arms around us both. I pulled one away from John and pulled her in closer. Behind us, Eric had looked at the ultrasound. He didn't know Marion and John's tragic past with fertility and being told she will never conceive again, but he seemed just as excited as I was.
"Congratulations you guys!" he cheered. I pulled away from them and stepped back.
I dropped to my knees in front of Marion's belly. She wasn't showing just yet, but I knew the little ones spirt could hear me.
"Hey cutie, we have waited so long for you to finally be here. I can't wait to meet you." I gushed to her stomach. My hands gently cupping her stomach.
"They are just going to adore you, Marty." Marion sniffed. Her happy tears continued to fall.
"I love them so much already." I smiled happily.
"Righto, kid. Boy or girl." John knelt down next to me. I put my hand over Marion's soft belly as she lifted the fabric of her shirt.
"Girl." I stated. I felt certain the growing baby was going to be a girl.
"That's what we think!" Marion gasped.
"Really?" I laughed out happily.
"Yeah!" John placed his large hand on top of mine.
"We have a girl's name picked out already though." Marion shrugged. Placing her own hand over ours.
"What is it?" Eric asked, his hand grasping my shoulder lovingly.
Marion looked me dead in the eyes and John squeezed my hand beneath his.
"Maree." John said softly.

Tears rained from my eyes again. I raised my spare hand to stifle a sob as it left my mouth. My body fell back against John who knelt behind me. His reflexes were quick as he caught me.

"It's beautiful." I managed to say in between my sobs. Mum would have loved that. I could picture the excitement in her face as if she were still here with us.

"We thought you'd approve." John pulled me into a tight bear hug. The scent of wood tingling my nose. He had been carving again. The crib he had spent years hoping to be filled would now be used.

"I love it." I whimpered.

"We couldn't have any other name for a little girl. Everything else just sounded too wrong." Marion laughed through her tears.

"I am so happy for you!" I stood shakily, pulling myself away from John.

"I have a good feeling about our little fighter." Marion gushed as she rubbed her own stomach.

I threw my arms around her and held her close Eric helped John up from behind us.

Dinner went quickly after the announcement was made, the happy mood filling the air with delight. The afternoon sun set in the distance.

We spent the evening discussing all things to do with pregnancy and children.

Eric sat next to me, beaming as he offered his own input into the different discussions.

He continued to smile for the remainder of night and was somehow still beaming when he laid down next to me in bed.

"They are going to be great parents." He whispered, pulling me close to his bare chest. He had started to sleep without a shirt on and I did not mind one bit. The delicious warmth radiated from his skin.

"They already are." I nuzzled my face into his warm embrace, inhaling deeply.

"I wish you could come to the city tomorrow." He gently raked a hand through my soft waves, threading his fingers through the ends. The wave of calm rolled over me with a welcome. I restrained myself from purring with delight.
"I'm sorry."
"It's alright. I want you to have a girly night with Charlotte. It will be good for you to have friends closer to you."
"I know." I said nervously, nuzzling deeper into his chest.

I closed my eyes and inhaled deeply. The scent of Eric's skin relaxing my body all over. I smiled against him. My eyes fluttered shut, the sweet allure of sleep swept me under.

## Chapter Twenty-Seven

"I love you."
Eric's goodbye played in my head as I vacuumed the already spotless floors. The hum of the machine made it hard to hear my own panicked thoughts. The house needed to spotless before Charlotte got here.
The majority of my morning after Eric left was spent on the phone to Kresley. She was doing well for herself, and I was proud of her for that. She spun tales of how the city was treating her and how she was ready to find someone new. It was great to hear her happy, my insides practically glowing with her joy.
I lit a candle on the coffee table in the loungeroom. The smell of coconut and lavender swirled in the air of the small room. The sun peaked its warmth inside. There was no rain forecast today which made me feel instantly calmer as soon as I heard the news reporter announce it. The thought of Eric driving alone in the rain and having an accident was enough to make me want to be sick. But I had followed Lydia's calming techniques and had managed to bring myself back relatively quick.
"Almost done." I announced to the dead silent air. The only thing left to do was straighten the couch.
My fingers glided over the yellow blanket. The memory of Eric wrapped up warmly in it with a book in his hands

brought a pang of pain to my chest. He had only been gone five hours and I already missed him dreadfully.
My phone buzzed loudly on the coffee table. The silent air now alert with the new sound.
*"I miss you already ha-ha."* It read. I grinned to myself. Blush warming my face.
*"I miss you too. Now, go have fun! x"* I responded before putting it back on the pine side table.
My gaze fluttered to the clock above the vase on the wall. The tall wildflowers reaching up toward it.
Five pm.
I had around two hours before Charlotte would arrive.
The jarringly loud buzz of my phone against the wood snapped my focus from the time.
I clicked it open.
*"Hey Marty! So, I'm like really bored. Would you like me to come earlier? My partner is going to drop me off so that we can have a drink together. I'll bring the wine!"* I read the message in Charlotte's bubbly tone.
*"Yeah of course ha-ha. Come whenever you like."* I typed back.
*"I'll get dressed and I'll see you in about say half an hour?"*
*"Sounds good to me!"* I sent back with a wine emoji.
She responded with a wine glass emoji back.
The strong scent of the candle filled my nose, whisking away my oncoming panic.
I scrolled through my phone to find a playlist I liked. I pressed play and let the gentle folk music play through the portable speaker on top of the fireplace.
My feet carried slowly to the picture of my mother amongst the flowers in the field. My heart ached to see her just one last time. To hear her laugh and tell me how much she loves me. The photo of my father next to her brought a fresh sting of tears to my eyes.
"I am so sorry." I whispered to them as survivors guilt filled my body, clutching at my lungs.

I needed to draw myself away from the photos. I went to the kitchen and began to make a platter of cheese, fruit and crackers. I organised them all on a wooden board I found under the sink and laid it down neatly on the coffee table. It looked inviting with the two wineglasses next to it. My stomach rumbled in hunger at the sight of the completed board. My mouth watered for a single carrot, but I forced myself to wait until Charlotte had arrived/.

The sound of tyres on the gravel outside drew my hunger from my focus. Cautiously, I moved to the front door and flicked on the porch light. Drawing a deep breath, I opened the door slowly before stepping out to greet Charlotte.

"Hey, girlie!" Charlotte called from the car as she clambered out of the passenger side.

"Hey!" I called back with a wave. My feet stood planted to their spot on the porch below me.

Charlotte kissed her boyfriend goodbye through the car window. She stepped back and turned to me. Her beige woollen cardigan twirled in the soft winter breeze. She held the emerald wine bottle tight in her fist as she hurried up the porch and out of the cold.

"It's absolutely freezing out here!" she noted before wrapping her arms around my neck.

"Come inside." I gestured to the open house behind me.

"Gladly." She chuckled before leading the way in.

Charlotte kicked off her white sneakers and gasped as she looked around the house.

"What?" I panicked. Everything looked neat to me. What had she seen?

"This place is beautiful!" she swooned. Her gaze taking in every corner of the home she could see. Light glistened in her eyes as she stood in awe.

"Oh, thank you." I said, relieved. My teeth nibbled at the lower lip nervously. My fingers itching to scratch my leg. The angry image of Linda entered my mind. I lifted my hand and shook her away. I wasn't bad again.

"Do you live here alone?" she asked as she wandered into the loungeroom, twirling to observe her surroundings. The open fire roaring in the wall. She gravitated toward it, letting it warm her jean covered legs.

"Yeah. Just me and Eric." I shrugged.

"That is so cute." Charlotte gushed. Her blue eyes dancing with adoration.

I laughed back, taking note that she was easy to please.

"Oh, I am starving!" she nearly shouted when she noticed the platter I had put out.

"Please" I pointed to the board "eat as much as you want."

"Gladly!" she chuckled, popping a grape in her plump glossy lips.

I smiled and sat down in my usual spot on the couch. Charlotte looked around the loungeroom once more but didn't say anything. Her gaze lingered on the photos of my parents.

"That's my parents." I declared from her side, her floral perfume filling the space around her. Stronger than the candle still burning on the side table.

"You look just like your mother." She pointed a perfectly manicured nail at a picture of my mother.

"I get told that all of the time." I sighed happily before moving back to the couch, holding a cushion to my chest for support.

Charlotte sat down gently beside me.

"Are you okay, Marty?" she cocked a thin eyebrow at me.

"Yeah why?" I asked, puzzled by her question.

"Just making sure you're alright." She pinched my leg softly, a small smile gracing her beautiful face.

Charlotte popped open the bottle of wine she had brought with her and poured each of us a full glass.

"To a new friendship." She toasted.

"To a new friendship." I repeated her toast.

She clinked her glass against mine and raised her glass to her plumped glossed lips, taking a long swig of the bubbly liquid.

I followed suite. The wine was sweeter than I was used to, but I preferred it so much more.

"What is this?" I almost gasped with bliss. My eyes wide with wonder.

"Moscato." Charlotte smiled before taking a cracker and cheese and placing them in her mouth.

"It's really nice." I said softly.

Charlotte looked like your average twenty-three-year-old woman. She wore a tight white shirt with a beige woollen cardigan over a pair of deep blue jeans. Her blonde hair had been loosely curled and was falling softly over her smoothly made-up face. She was truly beautiful. The type of girl that graced a magazine cover for a perfume advertisement. A pang of unease thumped in my stomach. I didn't put any effort into myself tonight. I wore a pair of black jeans with a floral black shirt, and I had scraped my naturally wavy hair into a messy ponytail as usual. The only thing that stood out were my white socks.

"I love your shirt! It's too cute. Very you though." Charlotte's voice brought me back to reality.

The fire crackled loudly.

"Oh, thank you. I love that cardigan. It looks so warm!" I smiled.

"It's too warm." She groaned before pulling it off her body. I watched as she folded it neatly and placed it on the arm of the chair behind her.

"I'm sorry. The fire heat is warmer than the ducted heater." I pointed to the roof above us.

"Oh! It's all good. Don't stress. I'm just not used to a woodfire. Our house is all ducted. It's nice to be near an actual woodfire again. My boyfriend, Rick, he has one of those fake ones that's like gas or something. It's not as good as the real thing." She all but sighed at the fire. I didn't realise it was uncommon to have one these days. I wouldn't survive without mine.

We spent the night snacking on the cheese platter and sipping the wine. We finished the bottle and I had to forage through the house to find another one. Marion had left one here once before, but where was the only issue. After a short battle with the pantry shelves, I found it hidden in the back behind the vinegar. I popped it open. It was quite bitter compared to the one Charlotte had brought with her, but it was still nice to drink.

"You're really pretty, Marty." Charlotte slurred drunkenly on her words.

"I have nothing on you! You're practically a goddess." I waved my half empty glass at her.

"Pfft." Charlotte snorted. "Nothing compared to you. You have this like real natural earthy vibe, you know?"

Charlotte had given me her whole life story from birth through to now. She told me how she hated her life here and how her friends were all fake and 'wannabe city girls' as she called them. She told me it was nice to be friends with someone 'normal'. She was very open with me, but I couldn't help but be closed off with her. I wouldn't tell her about my trip to the centre just yet. I knew to wait until I felt more comfortable.

"I should probably head home." Charlotte said as she looked up the clock.

"It is getting pretty late." I noted. The clock read nine fifty pm.

"I'll call Rick." She dialled her boyfriend, and he told her he was on his way.

Charlotte left at ten past ten. I hugged her goodbye and watched her leave from the porch outside. Leaving me all alone in my big old house.

I wasn't sure whether it was the wine or the thrill of a new person coming into my life that gave me a spurt of confidence, but I enjoyed it none the less.

I padded softly up the stairs. My eyes fixed on the door handle of the master bedroom.

I hadn't been in there in years.

My fingers shook as I wrapped them around the cold metal of the door handle. It creaked loudly as it turned in my palm. My heart thundered in my chest. My lungs constricting so no air could fight its way out. My throat

suddenly dry.
I pushed lightly on the door. The wood groaning stiffly with the motion. The scent of old dust and mildew flooded my nose. Everything in the room looked as if it hadn't been touched in months.
I guess John and Marion couldn't bring themselves to come in here either. I didn't blame them. It was eerily silent. Not a single gust of wind could be heard outside. Taking a single step through the threshold, my heart pounded in my chest. Fear overran my body, blood thundered in my ears
"They aren't here." I reminded myself out loud.
The blue duvet was coated in a thin layer of grey dust. Nothing was out of place. Just the same old bed that had been there since I was a kid and all the same furniture. The drawers by the adjoining bathroom called to me. I opened them slowly, prepared to flee at any given moment. Dust flew everywhere with the sudden movement. I coughed as it entered my mouth.
Inside the dresser, laid out flat were dad's old t-shirts. Without thinking I raised a worn grey one to my nose. Inhaling deeply. I swore I could still smell his strong spicy cologne deeply imbedded in the cotton of the shirt. A smile crept across my face and tears stung my eyes.
I sat with the shirt on the bed, sending more dust into the air.
"I miss you so much, dad." I whispered into the soft fabric. The second the words had left my mouth, a floorboard seemed to creak outside the door frame.
I disregarded it. Thinking it was nothing more than my mind playing tricks on me once again.
I threw the shirt down beside me. My heart heaved with the feeling of guilt. I shouldn't be here. They should be, not me. I was alone and I was terrified of being sent back

to the centre. I moved back to the other drawers on the other side of the room. These were mums. The old dark wood looked pale with dust. I opened the third one down. Her shirts folded the exact way dads were in his drawers. Untouched.

My fingers grazed over the soft fabrics in the draw, stopping on a single shirt. The navy-blue cotton soothing my saddened fingers. I pulled the shirt out and held it close. Tears pooled in my eyes. I spotted a bottle of perfume on top of the dresser. The same scent she had worn for years and years. Marion had told me how she wore it from the moment she turned seventeen. The bottle was near empty. I was surprised there was any left in there at all. Without hesitation, I took the small glass canister in my hand and sprayed the golden liquid onto the dark shirt. The familiar scent of her perfume crept into my nose. The tears fell harder at the scent. I sat back on the bed. My body collapsing in the mounds of dust that had formed.

"I miss you so much." I sobbed into the shirt.

Memories of being a child and running after mum as she danced her way through the field of wildflowers ran through my mind. Her soft smile and laughter as I caught up to her. She would pick me up and twirl me around with her. She would smile and hold me close as we spun in the afternoon sun.

"You are my favourite thing in the world." She would always tell me.

She would say it every morning before school and every night before bed. Some nights she would even sneak into my room late at night and curl up next to me. She would stroke my hair and sing to me as she comforted not only me but herself as well with the motion.

I missed her warmth next to me. The long nights I spent awake were the ones where I expected her to walk through my door and tell me to hush just like she used to when I cried. I would look up at the stars outside and imagine being right by her side down in the field star gazing. She would wrap me up in a coat and blankets and take me into the field where she would put out a blanket for us to sit. I would sit and she would pass me a hot chocolate, or a bedtime tea and I would sit in her lap or curled up right next to her with her arms around me tightly. She would point to the stars and tell me every constellation she could see. When it rained, she preferred to come into my room and put on an old folk cd and slow dance with me. Some days she preferred to just take me for a drive through the town and onto old country roads just so we could be alone together.

I wish I was old enough to have appreciated the moments more. I held them very dear to my heart. I longed to feel her soft rosebud lips against my forehead just one more time or to hear her voice telling me she loves me to the stars and back for the last time. I hated the fact that she was alone when she passed. I hated the fact that she didn't get to say a proper goodbye.

I sobbed into the shirt, drenching it with my tears. Every sniffle bringing more of her scent into my nose which only brought more heart broken tears from my eyes. She was my universe and I had to live in this whole new world I had made for myself alone. I knew deep in my core that she was right beside me at this moment. I knew she would be singing to me and patting my matted hair in my ponytail. I could picture her heart aching at the thought of me being so upset. She was probably crying along with me from where she was on the other side. My body began to ache with the raking of my sobs. The sweet allure of a numbing sleep drew me closer, and I slipped into the darkness.

## Chapter Twenty - Eight

I woke with a start, hoping that it had all been a nightmare. My heart sank as I realised it wasn't. I was still in their room.
"No more." I declared sitting up.
The sun was only just beginning to rise through the window outside.
I couldn't bear to harbour the pain of the memories any longer. I needed to clean out this room. I needed to make it fresh and new, no more pain.
My feet carried my tired body to my shower. My eyes were still puffy from my episode last night. I ran my plastic hairbrush through my matted hair, wincing at the pulling. Dust rained down in the light streaming through the window with each brush.
The warm water of the shower cleaned the filth from my body. The aroma of the lavender body wash replacing the old musk.
I dressed in a set of old loose pyjamas and made my way back to the room with storage boxes I had found in the spare room. Marion left them for when we were ready to clean out the room.
"No better time than the present." I mumbled.
I hurled them onto the bed.
I started with dad's dresser. I threw all his underwear and socks into a plastic bag and threw it out and into the

hallway. Then I put all his shirt's bar three I had chosen to keep for myself in a box. He didn't have a lot of clothes or belongings to pack away. It was mostly mum's various items that I needed to pack. I finished dad's drawers and moved over to mums. I didn't spend too much time packing up her belongings. It hurt too much to think about them. I threw all her belongings in boxes and dragged them into the spare room.

The sun had now fully risen in the morning's blue sky. Clouds threatened to cover the light, but it still poked its way through. The overwhelming amount of dust had gotten to me. I wrenched open the old window on the right. The morning breeze filled the room with an air of crisp freshness.

I vacuumed and dusted the room to the point where it looked brand new. The bin outside growing fuller and fuller with dust as I swept it away. I scrubbed the bathroom entirely and changed the old bedding on the huge bed in the centre of the room to a fresh set of sheets and clean duvet. I had even gone as far as to vacuum the mattress itself.

The room looked brand new by the time I had finished scrubbing. The sun was now high in the sky, time passing rapidly.

I sat softly on the bed. My head aching from moving everything from one room to another. My body fell back against the plush bed. The soft blanket I had thrown over as decoration soothed my tired skin. A sigh of pleasure left my mouth.

"Marty?" Eric's voice broke me from my delirious thoughts.

"Hi, honey!" I called back.

His footfalls fell hard as he hurried toward the master bedroom. He froze in the doorway at the sight of the bedroom.

"Wow." He cooed happily.

"I spent all morning cleaning it." I brought myself up to face him, wincing as my muscles screamed in protest at me moving.

"You should have waited. I would have helped you." He cupped my face in his hands, pressing his lips to mine.

"I missed you." I changed the subject, pulling myself back from him.

"I missed you too." He kissed my forehead swiftly before getting up to explore the bedroom. He opened the door to the bathroom.

"This is perfect." He whispered.

"We still have to move our things into here." I stood. My feet collapsed from under me. The mattress helping to catch me as I fell.

"Are you okay?" Eric asked, quick to help me up.

"Just sore, tired and hungry." I shrugged. He wrapped his hands around my arms.

"Have you eaten today?" his blue eyes searched mine.

"No, I didn't really have dinner either." I admitted.

"Marty!" he hissed.

"I'm sorry." My gaze dropped to the floor sadly. I didn't mean to disappoint him.

"No matter. Come on. Let's have lunch." Eric grabbed my hand and led me out of the bedroom toward the kitchen below.

A bunch of yellow sun flowers sat in a round clear glass on the dining table. The bright blooms illuminating the room.

"Mum sent them home for you." Eric explained.

"Oh, that was sweet of her! How was she?" I asked, taking a seat at the table.

"Really good" Eric beamed "She can't wait to meet you. She absolutely loves you already." He gushed.

Eric opened the refrigerator and pulled out butter and cheese. He moved to the bread box and pulled out two slices.

"She doesn't even know me." I laughed.

"I told her all about you and shown her some photos of you that I have. She thinks that you are just as beautiful as I do." He had his back to me as he prepared my sandwich. I toyed with the yellow petals from the flowers, pondering where he got the photos.

"Tell her I said thank you."

"Can do. How was Charlotte?" he asked.

"Really good." I responded. My mind drawing a blank. All I could remember from last night was crying over my parents. I looked down at my lap glumly. I couldn't tell Eric. It would only make him worry.

His tone was sweet as he sat my plated lunch down in front of me "Here you go, my love." His lips pressed against my frayed hair.

"Thank you." I forced myself to sound cheerful when in reality I felt anything but.

"Did you want to move the rest of our things into the new room today?"

"Yeah, let's get it over and done with." I spoke softly, trying to rid the pain from my voice.

I raised my sandwich to my mouth and took a bite. My stomach awakening at the taste of food entering my body. As I ate, Eric decompressed his entire day at his family's home. They had a great time full of laughs and joy. A stark difference to my depressing night after Charlotte had left. He told tales of how his dad would question him about me and then make fun of him when he saw Eric blush.

My heart ached to know what it felt like to have family days where you saw both parents. The only way I could do that would be to go to the cemetery. I hadn't done that in years. It hurt too much to think about going anymore.

It was going to be a long day.

## Chapter Twenty-Nine

The move into the new room had gone smoothly. We moved everything in and spent our first night together in there. Although I didn't sleep much. The thought of laying on my mothers' side of the bed was playing on my mind knowing how her and dad ended up. My mind would wander to where Eric and I would end up in an endless tormenting loop. Would I be able to keep him happy or would he turn on me and despise me? I would turn to face Eric and smile at his sleeping face. He looked so peaceful when he was asleep. I reached out a shaky hand to rub my thumb over his shaven cheek. His eyes popped open at my touch.
"Why aren't you sleeping?" he groaned tiredly, squeezing his eyes shut tight.
"I can't stop thinking of my mum." I admitted.
"Are you okay?" Eric asked, sitting up from his spot and looking directly into my eyes.
"I think I'm getting a bit panicky." I looked down at his hands where he clutched the blanket over his bare chest.
"I have an idea."
Eric moved from the bed and made his way over to my side.
"Here." He offered me a hand.
"Where are we going?" I took his hand in mine.
"Somewhere you'll feel safer. More at peace." Eric handed me a coat from the hooks on the back of the door and slid

his over himself. He slid on a pair of slippers and gestured for me to put mine on.

I followed him outside and out to the field. The harsh winter night air blew through my body. I shivered in the breeze.

"Why are we out here?" I hissed at Eric, gripping his hand tighter.

"We are going to your field."

"It's the middle of the night! You have work tomorrow."

"You are more important." He stated, ending the argument before it began.

Eric squeezed my hand as he found a shallow patch amongst the grass. The moon had appeared from its curtains of clouds and was beaming a pale light down to the ground surrounding us.

Eric moved his spare hand to the small of my back and held the other in his. I lifted my free hand to his shoulder, not knowing what else to do.

He began to sway slowly to a tune he played in his own head. I followed along with his motion. My body moving in time with his. Eric twirled me around with him. The brush of the grass below us crunched with our steps.

I moved myself into Eric's chest, burying my face into his embrace. My heartbeat steadied in my chest. The dance relaxing my body.

"Feel better?" Eric whispered into my hair.

"Much." I said, still muffled against his chest. Tears pricked at my eyes. The sweet gesture creating a whirlwind of emotions.

"Should we go back to bed?" he asked.

I nodded and he led me back to the house.

We slept with the curtains open so that the evening light would pour in. But there was no more evening light. Dark clouds had filled the sky once more. Another storm was rolling in.

I pulled my truck into Marion's driveway and turned off the ignition. She had messaged me in the morning and told me she was faking a sick day, so she called me straight away to come spend the day with her before John came home.

She didn't want to be alone, and I understood that completely. I hated being alone most of the time these days. After being by myself for so long and finally finding more people to spend my time with, I dreaded the moments I would be alone again. Eric was going to have a big day at work today, so I wanted to make him a nice dinner to come home to.

I walked quickly to the front door. Rain had begun to mist and drizzle down onto the cool morning air. Kids ran up the street in their rush to get to the school just down the road. I didn't even knock. Instead, just entering straight into the house and kicking off my shoes at the door.

"Hi love!" Marion called from the family room.

"Hey Maz!" I called back.

She sat under a blanket with a book in her hands on the large red couch. Her usually neat hair was a mess of waves around her head. She sported not a speck of make-up, yet she still looked just as beautiful as ever. A glow of happiness radiated from her skin.

"Come sit with me." she scooted over from her spot on the couch. I sat in the spot she had made, still warm from her body. She leant back to lay against me. I draped my arm over her shoulder as she nuzzled in closer to me.

"How are you feeling?" I rubbed my thumb up and down her bicep comfortingly.

"Good. I was just far too tired to look after the kids today." She puffed, waving her hand with a feign of exhaustion.

"I can imagine." I agreed, smiling at her motion.

"That and I missed my little Marty." Marion moved her head to kiss my hand.

"I missed you too." I cooed. She smiled up at me, her book still in her hands.

"Guess what I did yesterday?" I asked her.

"What?" she said, worry tainting her tone.
"I cleaned out the master bedroom."
Marion shot up in her seat and turned to face me. She held one hand to her budding stomach and the other took mine. She squeezed it tightly.
"Are you okay? How'd you go?" she asked worriedly.
"I'm fine. I don't need to go back to the centre or anything." I joked.
Marion looked at me blankly with her wide eyes.
"I'm fine. Trust me. Everything is in storage anyway in the spare room." I waved her away with a single hand.
"You should have said. I would have come and helped you!" Marion fretted.
"I didn't want to bother anyone. Besides I think I really needed to do it to accept the fact that they are *both* gone. It was something I had to do alone." I rubbed my thumb over her delicate hand.
"I understand." She sighed.
"I couldn't stop myself from taking this though." I reached into my jacket pocket and pulled out a piece of paper.
A small picture of mum, Marion and their father sat on mum's dresser when I was cleaning it. I knew Marion would appreciate it.
Marion's eyes glazed over with a sting of tears as she looked at the photo. She looked as if she was seventeen in the photo.
"Look at Papa!" she choked out.
"Is that Grandpa?" I asked, pointing at the greying man in the picture.
"Yes. That's my Papa. He was the sweetest man! He only ever did what was best for us, that man. He would have loved you! You should have seen him when he found out Maree was pregnant." She giggled to herself.
"What did he say?" I choked out a laugh.
"He went and brought all of these little baby things for you and he was so proud to be a grandpa."
"How did he pass, Aunt Marion?" I asked, trying to keep my voice light.

"Cancer" she said sadly "He didn't know he was sick until it was too late. He died about three months before you were born. I swear some nights I can feel him *and* your mother watching me." she pinched my cheek tightly.
I didn't pull away this time, I simply let her do it.
"I always feel mum around me."
"I can guarantee she is, my love. Just as John and I would be. God forbid anything like that would ever happen to us yet though." She squeezed my hand.
"Yeah, please don't leave me at all. I would have to go back to the centre if you left me."
Marion laughed and shook her head. Her eyes a mix of emotions.
"Want to see something cool?" she teased me.
"Of course." I answered eager to see what it was.
Marion lent her small frame over me to the side table. Her manicured fingers curling around the remote. She turned the TV on and changed the source to DVD.
My heart raced in my chest at the thought of what this might be.
"This better not be another funny cat video, Maz." I tried to joke to make myself feel easier.
Marion ignored me and pressed play on her remote.
The TV went black. An image burst onto the screen. A white bean shaped object appeared on the screen and a watery beat flooded from the speakers.
"What is that?" I asked Marion, puzzled by the image.
"That my dear, is your baby cousin." She grinned at the picture on the screen. Her hands cupping her belly whilst she watched the screen.
"No way." I breathed.
"Yes way." Marion chuckled.
A huffed laugh left my throat. Amazement filled my mind. The little bean on the screen seemed to be floating amongst the darkness. A little ball of light. This baby was going to be the most loved child in the entire world.
"It looks like a little jellybean." I blurted out. I gestured a little bean with my thumb and index finger.

"John says the same thing." Marion laughed, amused by my answer.

"Going to be a cutie aren't you, little jelly." I turned and spoke to Marion's belly.

"Jelly?" Marion cocked an eyebrow in confusion.

"That's their new nickname." I extended my hand to feel Marion's stomach.

Marion's hands met mine and she pushed them lightly against her.

"What a year." She breathed.

"Yeah, What a year." I repeated.

*Chapter Thirty*

I drove home around noon. The rain had slowed its drizzle and was nothing more than a light mist in the air. The drive home consisted of a happy smile on my face and happy music blaring through my truck. I sang along to all the songs I knew joyfully, still buzzing about the concept of meeting my cousin.

The house was cold as I entered. The crisp winter air had made its way inside. Hanging up my coat, I decided to just turn the ducted heating on. It was too much effort to light the fire. I sat down on the couch. The allure of sleep clouding my mind.

I woke to the floor of the kitchen creaking. I glanced at the clock. Four forty-five. Eric would be home any minute. The floor in the kitchen creaked again.

"Eric?" I called.

No one answered.

"Eric, this isn't funny." I laughed as I stood. The blinds to the kitchen were open but I couldn't see a reflection of anyone in them.

The floor creaked louder this time. I jolted with panic. Who was here?

"Hello?" I called softly out to kitchen.

Again, no one answered.

I inhaled deeply. Trying to find the courage to look through the door frame.

"There's no one here, Marty. You know that. You'll see."

I said softly to myself in an attempt to calm down my racing heart. I took a step forward to the arch way of the kitchen.
I let out my breath and poked my head through the door frame.
There he stood. Tall and rugged. His wild eyes staring through me.
My father.
"No." I whispered to myself. My hands racing up to grip my already messed-up hair.
"Marty!" he said happily as he made his way over to where I was frozen in the archway. He grinned at the sight of me. Pleasure growing in his eyes. His arms outstretched to embrace me.
"You aren't real." I muttered. I was doing so well. How was he back? I wasn't stressed or upset at all! It wasn't possible. I was normal again.
"No!" I screamed as he walked up to me quickly. My throat grew dry. I stepped back into the lounge room, falling harshly over my own two feet. My back hitting the ground hard. Pain flowed up through my lower spine. A scream burning my throat, yet to be released.
"What are you going on about?" he questioned my response to seeing him "Don't you want to see your old man?" he furrowed his thick brows.
I scurried backwards on the shabby carpet underneath me. My skin burning in the motion.
"You aren't real!" I cried. Panic began to overtake me. I blinked hard to see if he would disappear again.
"Well, I am as real as that boy that's now living here." He pointed to the boxes we had left in the corner. I flinched at the memory of his hand slapping my face in his fit of rage.
"Marty, what did they do to you?" he asked sadly as he stared down at me. His strong hand twitching at his sides.
"You aren't real, Dad. You're just a figment of my mind. A panic response." I put my hands up to my head again. My fingers pulling at my roots.
"I am real. I'm here, Martha." He said softly. Dad stepped

closer to where I was on the floor. "I went into town to see you for the little café party. Didn't you see me?" he tried to soothe me with his voice, but my panic was too strong to be calmed.

"I was doing so well!" I screamed. Why was he here? I was finally happy again!

"What are you on about, kid?" he bellowed, throwing his strong arms up in anger.

"Leave me alone!" I screeched loudly. My back hit the windowpane as I used it to help myself up.

I stood shakily and my eyes darted to the door. I looked back at dad before sprinting to my escape.

Dad's strong arms ripped me back the same moment I reached for the handle. Pain radiated from my spine.

"You aren't real!" I screamed again as he wrenched me back from the door like a doll. I kicked my legs out, fighting to free myself from his tight grip. He pushed me against the hallway wall. The same place he held me the last time.

"I am real, Marty! My god! What is wrong with you! What did they do to you?"

"You died! You died in a fire!" I squealed. My legs kicking against his shins. Fingers clawing at his face.

"I did not, Martha!" he groaned from the force of my struggle.

"I want you to leave me alone!" I ordered as he held me back to him.

"No!" he grunted as he struggled to hold my struggling body.

"Yes, I have come so far! You aren't real!" I shouted again, continuing to wriggle for my freedom.

The front door flew open.

"Marty, what the hell is going on? I came to bring you the DVD of the ultrasound to show Eric and all I can hear outside is screaming." Marion called. She was by herself as she closed the door behind her. She placed her handbag neatly on the entry table before looking up and spotting us. Dad's grip slipped as he hoisted me from the wall to stand

in front of him.
Dad tensed behind me he put a hand over my mouth so I couldn't speak. The taste of stale dirt filled my lips as I screamed from behind them.
Marion turned her full attention to dad and me in the hall. I kicked harder against him to get free. My nails digging into his arms.
"I'm not real, Marion?" dad spat venomously at her. His blue eyes ablaze with madness and deep hatred,
"No. You can't be." Marion just about fell over. She fell back against the door in disbelief. Her small hands gripping the doorframe for support as she shakily stood back up.
"Here I am!" he gripped me tighter against him. My ribs felt like they were about to snap with the pressure of dad's arms around them. I screamed for Marion to run but it was too muffled for her to make out.
I tried to wriggle my way out again but couldn't, his forceful grip on me got even tighter.
"You told my own daughter that I had died. You took her away from me, Marion! You filled her head with those heartless lies. You don't do that. Not to me." Dad's deep voice boomed.
"You were dead, Richard! You were dead over ten years!" she gasped. Her small hands cupping her perfect mouth.
"I'm truly surprised, Marion. Didn't you know I faked it? I know our sweet little Marty here told you all about me." He admitted. He laughed manically at her shock. His grip on my loosened slightly as I fought for air. Air rushed harshly down my airways as I gulped it down. Tears stung my eyes.
"Why?" she asked. Her eyes grew as wide as saucers in fear. Her skin blanched white as the blood drained from her face.
"You know why!" he growled.
"You really did kill her, didn't you! You sick fuck!" Marion was in shock. Her small hands flew up to her aghast mouth. The colour draining from her skin

"Good work, Marion. Would you like a gold star?" Dad threw me behind him with force as he faced Marion himself. My tossed body fell hard the wooden floor and my head bounced back against the corner panel of the wall. My forehead hit the ground hard. A headache blazed through me. Blood gushed from the fresh wound on my head. The world began to spin around me.
"Why?" Marion screeched. She was frozen to her spot.
"She was going to leave me, Marion. Leave me all alone and take my daughter away from me. She was going to make that other man Marty's father. My own daughter was going to belong to some other man." He took a step toward her.
"Good." Marion spat at him "You are a pig of a man. I truly had hoped you burnt horribly in that fire." Her face contorted with a deep rage.
"But I didn't. Would you like to know just how I killed her?" he laughed manically. He cocked his large head to the side and stared her down.
"How?" Marion asked strongly, her hands balling into a tight shaky fist.
Dad stood up straight, a glint of silver from the afternoon light in the back of his dark jean's waist band caught my attention through the down pour of blood covering my face.
"Well, it was pouring rain and she was on her way back to take Marty from me. I was not just going to let that happen. I wasn't going quietly" He shook his head.
"What did you do, Richard?" she pressed. Her voice staying strong. Anger began coursing through it viciously.
"I jumped out in front of the fancy new car I had just brought her, and she swerved into the tree to avoid hitting me. I could see her scream as she turned the wheel. She didn't die in the crash though. She survived it."
"Dad?" I panicked at the sight of the gun hidden in his pants. I tried to move closer to get a better look, but my head burned every time I moved. I was stuck, rotted to my place on the floor.

"Shut up, Martha!" he barked back at me on the floor and turned his attention back to her. "I pulled the door open and pulled her out as much as I could. She begged me to help but I didn't. Would you like to know what I did instead?" he stepped toward Marion. His chest rising heavily with each step.

"What did you do, Richard?" Marion asked through her angry tears.

"I took out the little pocketknife she brought for my nineteenth birthday. You remember that little knife? Well, I stabbed her. Right here. In her whored little heart. Then I fled. Ran off to the city to fake my death. I kidnapped some man off the street and burnt the place to the ground." He pointed to his heart area, snarling.

"You are an actual fucking psychopath. You always were!" Marion screeched as she stepped back away from him.

"No. You are Marion" he pointed at her, his hand shaking with relentless rage. "You should never have come here. You should have just stayed away like I warned."

"All these years, those notes were from you?" Marion's voice was laced with fear.

"Who else knew you like that?" dad laughed at her.

"I thought I was going crazy." She gasped with realisation.

"Nope, but you ignored my warnings. Now, Marion, you are going to pay."

"Richard, please. If you didn't want Marty in the first place, why put her through all of this now?"

"I never wanted kids. Dirty little things but there was something about Marty. So easy to manipulate. So easy to turn her for my will.

She may have saved me, Marion, but she can't save you."

Dad reached back for the gun, and I leapt up to him. A wave of adrenaline coursed through me. My hands closed around the barrel of the gun. Dad's fingers eager to wrench mine off. We both fought for the weapon, but dad was too strong for me. He tossed me off with a hit of his elbow back into my throat. I fell back hitting my face again. Marion had moved to the door. Her hand gripped tightly on the brass handle.

I screamed for dad to stop but he didn't. Just as I stood back up, the gun fired loudly, and Marion fell back toward the door. Her body hitting it hard as she fell against it. Scarlet blood streaked down after her. She rolled over to her back with thick red blood flowing from the wound on her spine. I dropped to my knees at the sight of her.

"No!" I screamed, frantically crawling past dad to reach for her. She reached a weak hand out to me with her big blue eyes wild with pain and held mine tightly. Tears streamed down my face as I watched the life leave her eyes. Her small chest rose one last time only to fall softly as if her soul was leaving her body.

"No! Please stay with me" I sobbed "this is all my fault." I put my head down onto her chest. My tears wetting her shirt as I cried.

"Aunt Marion, please! Stay with me. I can't lose you!" Dad's strong rough arms hoisted me up from the ground. He put a large hand around my mouth as I tried to scream. Marion's life had drained out of her body. I screamed into dad's hand as he dragged me though the kitchen.

A car door closing echoed from out the front of the house. "Shit." Dad muttered. He thrust us toward the back door as I kicked and screamed the entire way out. The gun fell from dad's grip as he hurled me forward with him. He shut the door just as the person opened the front entrance. I heard them scream. The noise enough to curdle blood. I kicked the back door harsh as we stepped off the step. The knock echoing through the house. Alerting anyone that I was still here. That I was still alive, for now.

Dad dragged me quickly to the field of wildflowers as I struggled to release his grip on me. I landed with a hefty thud as he threw me down on to a dense patch of blooms and knelt next to me with his cold hand still over my mouth.

"Shut up, Martha or I swear to God. I will kill you too."

He sneered threateningly. He stood over me, grabbing my ankles and dragged my body to the edge of the forest where he let me go. My heavy legs dropped hard on the sticks of the forest floor. I screamed for help. My voice trembling with fear.

"You have two choices. Come with me now, Martha or I kill you. You choose." He stood over me breathing heavy. His chest heaving with the motion.

"I'm not going anywhere with you. You're a monster!" I said through gritted teeth. My body ached after being dragged through the open field. I struggled to find my breath. My lunges singed with every breath I took. The image of Marion's lifeless body vivid in my head. Tears stung my eyes. This was all my fault. Dad knelt over me and placed a knee hard into my chest. A small whimper escaped me.

Dad's fingers danced over his chest as he ripped a piece of fabric from his dirty long sleeve before forcing the rag into my mouth. No matter how much I threw my head around it was no use. The acidic taste of sweat filled my mouth as he shoved it in further. My muffled cries barely audible in the damp forest air.

"You made your choice." He shrugged and dragged me further into the woods by my arms with no hope of removing the gag. I squinted to the distance. I could see Eric in the distance running out of the house toward us. Tears fell from my blood covered eyes at the sight of his panicked run.

Sticks and debris tore at my bare skin as my shirt lifted as I was dragged across the damp and sharp forest floor. I kicked out at the earth with all my strength. Trying to find anything to slow us down.

Dad's attention turned to an animal running toward us in the forest. His body growing tense with the noise.

Eric's voice echoed in the forest around us, full of panic as he screamed out my name from somewhere behind. I took this as my chance. Dad's grip on my arms loosened as he assessed his next move. His eyes looking around the forest for the way to go. I wrenched my arms down with all the strength I had left. My body aching from being torn apart against the rough earth beneath us. He stumbled from the impact my feet fumbled beneath me as managed to get up quickly and sprint away from where I left him roaring with rage, heading further into the deep of the forest. I couldn't run toward Eric; dad would kill him on sight. I spat the filthy fabric from my mouth as I ran. Throwing it away into the dense brush. Not hesitating to remove the spit from my mouth after it.

The leaves crunched under me as I then ran deeper into the thick forest. The damp smell of soil running with me as a stomped through the mud. Branches raked my skin as I hurled myself through them repeatedly. The trees getting thicker the deeper in I went. The sky above darkening with each second.

"You cannot escape me, Martha! I will always find you." dad called menacingly from somewhere behind me. I couldn't run much further. My legs began to slow as my feet barely lifted off the ground. Exhaustion overtook me. My lungs burning like fire. My bones ached from within. My entire being was aching, and my head wound made me dizzy. I tripped over a low-lying branch and fell face first into the damp earth. The wound on my forehead had burst and reopened, and the blood began to drip slowly into my eyes. My vision becoming blurred. Faint colours danced in my sight.

"You always did like being outside, kid." Dad was standing only feet from me. He towered over me as I wriggled away in fear. I reached for anything I could to help me get away from him. I pulled myself forward with a small tree, but it was no use. Dad had caught me. He rolled me over on to my back and sat on top of me. His heavy weight crushing me back into the frigid damp earth. The trees swayed furiously in the wind of the oncoming storm. Their green leaves falling around us.

"I didn't want to do this, Martha. But you left me no choice." He grunted as he wrapped his strong hands around my neck. His thumbs closing in tightly against my throat. He shook his greying hair out of his dirt covered face as he stared blankly into my eyes.

"Please, Dad. Please don't do this!" I tried to beg as his cut off my airways. I scratched at his hands with my nails and kicked out my feet to no avail.

"You are just too much like your stupid mother." He grunted again. I began to feel dizzy with the lack of oxygen. I scratched at his hands around my neck again, but it was no use. I let them go. My hands fumbled around me for anything I could use to knock him off. He loosened his grip to let me breath whilst he talked, keeping me alive just long enough to hear him out. My airways choking for the air I desperately needed. The storm was coming over the forest. Darkness overtook the sky.

"Nothing but a nasty little whore. That's what you are Martha. A little whore. You will never amount to anything. You will run yourself into the ground at that old Café!"

"At least I will never turn out like you. A god damn psychopath!" I spat as he loosened his grip further to hear my response.

"Oh, that it just perfect, Marty. You sound just like your bitch of a mother." he laughed deeply. The malicious tone ripping me with fear.

He looked at me with wild eyes as he closed his grip on my throat tighter again.

"I loved you more than anything." He grunted.

"You don't know what love is." I managed to hiss.

"Oh yeah? Then what is love, Martha? You really think that boy will love your messed up head?" he growled out a dark chuckle before removing one of his hands from my throat. His knuckles collided with my cheek. The warm rush of blood filled my mouth, leaking from the sides of my lips. Tears tried to fall as I sobbed. The sound of my father laughing only deepening the sadness.

"You promised you wouldn't hurt me." I choked out in between my gasps for air.

"I promised you nothing, kid."
My heart broke even further in my chest as if it were possible. His cruel smile wavered above me. I wasn't going to let this be the last thing I seen. I raked my hands through the earth around us trying to find even the smallest thing I could use. My fingers felt a small sharp rock buried beneath the shallow soil and curled my fist around it. I mustered the last of my strength and whacked him square in the temple with it with all I had left in me. He roared in pain and let me go to put his hands to his gapping head wound. Scarlet blood poured onto his dirt covered face. I gasped for air under him. He looked down at me. His blue eyes wild with hatred. I hoisted my knee up under him. Thrusting it harshly into his groin. He roared with pain once more and fell to the side. I stood shakily above him. My foot connecting with his ribs as I kicked him. I stood back. The rock still in my fist. Taking careful aim, I threw it perfectly at his other temple. Another roar ripped through the silent forest air.

I needed to escape again. Rain began to fall harshly through the cover of the trees. A loud clap of thunder burst from around us. The ground shook with the vibration. I sprinted as fast as I could to the edge of the forest near the house. The ground shook under me as I hurried away from my doom. I could feel my father's presence behind me. I screamed Eric's name in the hope that he was still searching for me. My name echoed back in the distance. Dad's panting came up closely behind me. Birds flustered in a frenzy from their nest, cawing into the sky with warning.

"Please just let me go." I cried out. I leapt forward over a low-lying branch only to be pulled back by his hand on my arm. He was far too strong for me to wrench myself from his grip. He moved his grip up my shoulder and in one fluid motion, I was thrown back against the hard earth. My breath left me silently. Rain began to flood on the ground causing a musky scent to fill my nose.

I looked up pleadingly at my father who was breathing heavily above me. His eyes wild with anger.

"I'm sorry" I grunted "I'll come with you. We can forget about all of this. Please, dad." I was desperate to do anything to save myself at this point, but I knew it was no use. I knew this was my end.

"No more." He whispered as he grabbed my throat once more. This time he held it harder. His fingers crushing my neck between themselves. The light of the sky began to fade and become fuzzy in my blurred vision. The tall trees swirled into a mess of blazing green colour. Dad's face was contorted with concentration as he directly looked into my eyes. Anger raged inside them.

"Say hi to your filthy mother for me. You deserve to be with her, Marty. I never even wanted you. You know that, right? Your stupid mother had always wanted a baby, but I didn't want that. All she ended up doing was giving me a weapon to use against her. That's all you are, Martha. A toy in this messed up love story. You would have never found love. You would have just whored yourself out just like your slut of a mother. So good luck up there, Martha. This won't take much longer. I promise. You will be with her soon enough." He looked me dead in the eyes as he spoke his harsh words.

"Please stop, daddy. I'll be good I promise" I mouthed, feeling my end coming. The edges of my vision began to cloud with darkness as my lungs burned with fire. My eyes stung with the blood and dirt that had rained down into them. Tears cleaned my face as they streaked down it. Drops of water began to fall through the trees overhead even heavier. Lightning illuminated the sky through the dense branches.

'I'm coming home, Mumma.' I thought to myself. I looked up at the sky peeking through the heavy trees. The dark storm clouds moved quickly overhead.

The boom of a gunshot echoed through the thin foggy air and dad's grip loosened from around my neck. Blood flowed from his dirty grey shirt and dropped down hotly onto my face. His eyes rolled back into his head as he fell forward onto me. His body dropped and his last breath left his body softly.

I continued to gasp for air, pushing his heavy corpse off me. My lungs burned with the harsh rush of cold air as I inhaled. I rolled to my side. Gulping down as much air as I could. My fingers massaging where his hands had crushed my throat as I struggled to breathe.

"Marty!" I heard my name being called. I didn't look around to see where the voice was coming from though. My ears began to ring loudly, and my body ached in pain. The wound on my head stinging from the dirt and earth that had filled it along with the pouring rain. My throat burnt with every breath I took.

I closed my eyes with sheer exhaustion. The allure of darkness filled my mind as I laid back down against the cold earth. The last thing I saw was my father's cold dead face staring at me with the whites of his eyes. His mouth twisted into a gaping hole of shock. Blood trickled from his mouth into his grey stubble and onto the dark soil below. Rain fell harder onto my tired skin. I felt hands touch my body and lift me to the sky. The allure of the black darkness overtook me, and I fell into it happily.

I came to as Eric carried me through the field of wildflowers. Red and blue lights flashed in my vision as he carefully stepped. People ran past us into the forest and voices called for me. Sirens blared in the distance
I blinked up at Eric whose face was wet with tears. The rain had begun to pour down on us but that didn't stop him. My eyes felt heavy as I struggled to keep them open
"Eric." I went to say his name, but I couldn't. Instead, I moved my head against his arm weakly.
He looked down at me, almost dropping me in shock. He fell to his knees in the field and held me close to his chest.

"I thought I had lost you." He lifted my chest to his as he sobbed into my dirty branch ridden hair. I nuzzled in softly to his soft neck.
"You didn't. You couldn't." I breathed.
"We should have believed you." He wiped the hair from my dirty head wound. He shook his head at his choices. They didn't know he was alive. Dad was just too smart. I wouldn't have believed me either.
"It's okay." I choked out. The metallic taste of blood filled my mouth.
"I love you." He cried to me.
"I love you too." I responded as loudly as I could. The words sounding more of a whisper than anything. He held me tighter as more people came toward us.
His misty blue eyes now red from tears he had shed.
"Now stay with me okay. I can't lose you again. Promise me you'll stay with me." He sniffed.
"I promise, Eric."
"Good." He smiled through his tears.
"It's over now." I assured him. I raised an arm with all the strength I had and cupped his prickly cheek. Black stubble had begun to grow from his pale angular jaw.
"It is." He smiled down at me.
The wildflowers grazed my skin as I smiled up at him. The intoxicatingly sweet scent calming me.
I was finally at peace…

**Acknowledgements:**

I would like to thank every single one of you for purchasing this book and supporting my dream, you have no idea how much your support means to me.

I would like to take this time to thank every single member of my family for listening to me babble on about how badly I wanted to be a writer and for supporting me through it all. You are my reason for living and creating the life I have.

Thank you to my friends who have supported me since day one, you know who you are and how much I love and thank you.

Thank you to Emma and Leica for proofreading my work and for being kind with any criticism you had.

To my beautiful Ben, I would like to thank you the most for your never wavering support. Words cannot express how deeply grateful I am to have you and your support. Thank you for wiping my tears when I am too stressed or holding me close when I can't breathe. My love for you is endless and this book would not be what it is without you. So, thank you, sweet boy.

To my mums and dads, thank you. I am so hopeful that I have made you proud with this book and I can honestly say that I would not be here today without your love.

To my bestie, thank you. There is no words to describe just how much you mean to me. Your never-ending love and praise were what got me through this journey, and I am grateful to have you closer by the end of it. You are my favourite person, and you always will be. Thank you for teaching me how to love and how to receive love in return.

Jasmine Styles is an indie author from Regional Australia who is pursuing her lifelong dream of being an author. When Jasmine isn't writing, she is spending time with the loved ones she holds closest, reading or buying way too many books, blasting music as loud as she can and going to any live concert she can.

CPSIA information can be obtained
at www.ICGtesting.com
Printed in the USA
BVHW041159240922
647852BV00022B/164